I0775404

# LeyGuards, Faespells,

## and Other Things That Breach the Veil

The Leyward Stones, Book 2

# Crystal Crawford

© 2022 Crystal Crawford, first published in serial format on as Part 2 (Episodes 38-65) of *Macchiatos, Faerie Princes, and Other Things That Happen at Midnight (The Leyward Stones, Season 1)*.

E-book and paperback formats published in 2023.

All Rights Reserved. No part of this publication may be reproduced, distributed, or transmitted in any form or by any means, including photocopying, recording, or other electronic or mechanical methods, without the prior written permission of the publisher, except in the case of brief quotations embodied in critical reviews and certain other noncommercial uses permitted by copyright law. For permission requests, contact ccrawford@ccrawfordwriting.com.

*This is a work of fiction. Any resemblance to actual events or persons, living or dead, is entirely coincidental.*

Cover art by Jason Crawford / Fierce, Inc.

# Map of Faeside
## Before the First Dark War

# Map of Faeside
## Present Day

# CONTENTS

# Chapter 1

# THE BLACK ABYSS

*Ayla*

A few weeks ago, in my safe little job at the café where my biggest concern in life was getting through high school unscathed by drama, I wouldn't have imagined that *anything* could have convinced me to leap headlong through a Fae portal into the dark and dangerous unknown of the Void.

But now, as I'm plummeting into it *yet again* to rescue someone I love, I realize how many reasons I have now to brave this danger. Grandpa. My parents. Reina, Callan, Madison, Rory, Champ, even Striker. I would risk this for any one of them... and I have. But Jordan—oh, Jordan. I would leap into the Void a million times over, if I knew for sure it would save you.

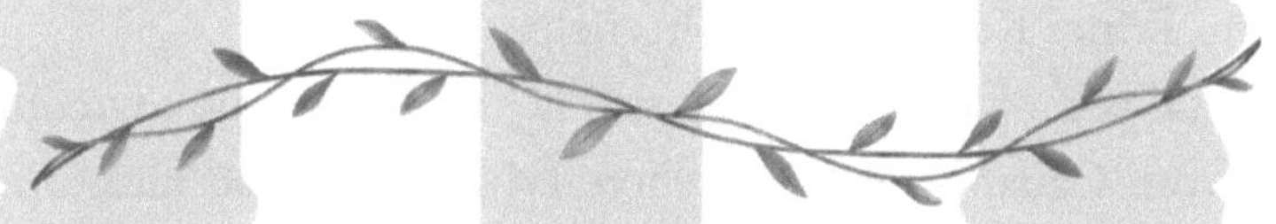

***One Week Earlier (just after leaping through the breach behind the cabin)***

The sound of Striker fighting the hounds cut off abruptly as the darkness of the Void swallowed me. The shimmering breach behind me snapped shut, taking with it the last of the light—my last tie back to Earthside. I hit the hard ground and stumbled. At least I'd managed to stay on my feet this time.

The darkness pressed in on me from every side, absolute and somehow tangible. I swore I could feel it, cold and clammy, resting on my skin. The two backpacks of supplies I carried—mine and Striker's—hung heavy from each of my shoulders. I'd get back and neck cramps from carrying them for long, for sure, but at least I would have supplies.

Not that I was sure what to do with them, or how to make camp in a place like this, even if I wanted to. I was terrified to move. Without seeing what was around me, I had no way of knowing I wasn't about to walk off a cliff... or into something worse, like the Veil-Dearg I'd met here just hours before. Or possibly five *days* before, according to how long Striker said I'd been missing before I reappeared Earthside.

*Five days.* I hadn't had time to fully consider the strange way time moved in the Veil before leaping right back into this place. What if the days were already speeding by Earthside as I stood here? And my friends, wherever they were, and Jordan... was time speeding by for them, too? The familiar claws of panic dug into my chest.

I forced a breath. I couldn't let myself worry about that now. Striker had said time moved strangely in *some* parts of the Veil. Maybe I was worrying about nothing. Either way, I couldn't stand here in the dark, panicking. I had to find Prince Kaizyn and get his help.

The metal rod of the ward key still lay warm against my collarbone, hanging from Callan's necklace where I'd left it. It had kicked me back Earthside before—just in time to save me from the Veil-Dearg. It was a relief knowing I had a key to reactivate the breach, assuming it would work again if I needed it to. But I couldn't go back Earthside, yet. This time, I had come here for a reason.

I eased Callan's necklace from beneath my shirt, careful not to touch the key, and lifted up the smooth stone. The stone that Callan said would lead me to Prince Kaizyn.

At first I couldn't see the stone at all—I couldn't even see my own hand in front of me—but as my fingers closed tight around it, it grew warm beneath my touch.

And then it glowed.

It was faint, all things considered, barely more than the glow of a cell phone screen, but there in that dark abyss, it may as well have been a beacon. I stared at it for one long, grateful moment, eyes stinging and watering from the light, before I realized if *I* could see the light, so could anything else. I gasped and shoved the stone back beneath my shirt.

As it settled against my skin, the stone's warm glow—which was now muted by my shirt—intensified into a hum. Then I felt it, a strange pull in my chest, like someone had tied a string around my heart and tugged.

*This way.*

It was wordless but unmistakable. I took a cautious step in that direction, breathing a small sigh of relief when I didn't fall off any unseen cliffs.

As I stepped, the stone's hum purred a little, almost like it was pleased, and a tiny wave of pleasant warmth surged out over my skin, like being wrapped in a blanket fresh from the dryer.

A reward, maybe, for moving in the right direction?

I stopped, a little unsettled by this magic. The stone felt *too* eager to lead me to the prince—if that's even where it was taking me. I'd watched enough fairy tale movies to know that magic this comforting was usually a trap.

But Callan had given me the stone, and though I didn't trust anything else about this place or its Fae magic in the least, I trusted Callan. And since I was low on options at the moment, I would have to just choose to continue to trust him... and the strange stone still shooting warm fuzzies through me with every step I took in its chosen direction.

How much I could trust the prince on the other end of this magic, however, was yet to be seen.

I took a few more cautious steps into the darkness, every step preceded by a tremor of fear that I might be about to step off of or into something unknown, and every step *followed* by a pleased purr and hug of warmth from the stone.

*I'm going to get murdered by some kind of cuddly woodland creature at the end of this path, I just know it.*

But that was irrational—I was far more likely to be murdered by a Veil-Dearg. Or a Fadehound. Or a Selkblood. Or a dozen other nightmare creatures I hadn't discovered yet, who were all probably hovering in the darkness, staring at me, waiting for their chance to pounce.

I suppressed a shiver.

Striker had said he would come find me as soon as he was able, but I wasn't certain how the breach magic worked. Did it open to the same place in the Veil every time? And even if it did, would Striker be able to open it without the key I carried?

I hoped he had his own LeyGuard ways of finding me, because I wasn't planning to wait around in the dark alone. I needed to find Prince Kaizyn, as quickly as possible. Once I found him, he could hopefully keep whatever else lived in this place from killing me. I adjusted the two heavy backpacks on my shoulders, took one long, steadying breath, and strode quickly in the direction of the stone's pull.

Something to my left hissed.

I froze. My heart hammered double-time as I held my breath, listening. I heard nothing, now—but that could just mean that whatever made the noise knew I was onto it, and was hiding.

My chest tightened in panic.

What in the world was I *doing* in here? Why had I ever imagined, even for a second, that I could navigate this terrifying, dark abyss to find Prince Kaizyn *alone*?

I never should've come through without Striker. I should've run, gotten away from the hounds, and figured out the rest later.

The darkness closed in on me. My breaths came tight, shallow, like I couldn't draw in enough air, and I felt suddenly claustrophobic.

I had to get *out.*

I snatched up the leather cord of Callan's necklace, fumbling for the key, to escape back Earthside—then clarity hit me like a sledgehammer, and I froze again.

What was I *doing?* I couldn't leave. I needed to find Kaizyn, so he could help me rescue Jordan, find my friends, save my parents. I needed to keep moving forward.

This place was doing weird things to my head.

The panic still crushed in so hard, I could hardly breathe. How was I supposed to save anyone else, if I could barely survive here *myself?*

Then I heard Striker's words in my mind: *You want to be brave? A hero? Then be one. No one can stop you. It only takes the courage to do what's right.*

Courage. I could have that, couldn't I? I could muster it. Or at least I could try.

I pictured Jordan's face, then Reina's smile, Grandpa's keen brown eyes, Callan's smirk, Madison's sassy hands-on-hips stance, my parents—smiling, as they were before, rather than unconscious as I'd last seen them. I took a shaky breath. *For them*—I could do this for them. But not stumbling blind. I needed light. Even if it might draw monsters to me, I had to risk it, or I'd never make it another step. At least with some light, I'd see what was coming for me.

I forced one more slow, deep breath, and drew the stone carefully back out from beneath my shirt.

*Now what?* The stone's glow spilled light between my fingers, illuminating my hands, but the darkness in the Void was so thick the light didn't penetrate much further than that. If I was going to move forward, I needed to at least see what I was walking into—or what might be stalking up to *me.* I held the stone tentatively outward, swallowing down a lump of fear, and scanned for the source of the hiss.

A dozen shimmering eyes glinted back at me.

My heart stopped for a beat. Snakes—or something close to it. Six of them. And big. Like anaconda big. Scattered around me in a loose semicircle. And every single one of them was staring right at me.

My heart restarted and shot off into a gallop.

They slithered closer.

Were these venomous? How would I know? And what would I do about it, if they *were* and one of them bit me?

*I'm going to die, right here in the black abyss.* Would anyone ever find my body? Would they even know I was dead? *Oh.* Kaizyn would know, because if I died, so would he. And if he died, Teionyr—and Jordan—might be lost, too. This was bigger than just me now. I had to be careful.

Should I use the ward key and try to breach out of the Veil? Maybe I could come back later, with Striker, and try again?

But my heart resisted that idea—I'd already taken the plunge, was already here, and every step backward was another moment wasted in trying to save Jordan or my parents.

I took a breath and stepped backward, keeping my hand outward so the snakes' eyes stayed within the weak glow of the stone. Maybe I could find a way around them.

The snakes were close enough to leap, but they seemed mostly curious. One of them flicked a forked tongue and tilted its head. Its eyes narrowed.

It coiled as if to lunge.

A pang of fear and sharp regret shot through me as I reached for the ward key—

A comet of flame barrelled toward me from the darkness.

I ducked into a tight ball, praying a frantic plea—I was certain I was about to die, after all, by incineration if not by venom.

The comet skidded to a stop in front of me and growled.

*Growled?* I peeked out through my fingers and gasped.

Standing between me and the snakes, back arched and hackles raised, was some kind of scorpion-cat monstrosity the size of a Great Dane... made entirely of pure flame.

The creature flicked its head to the side at my gasp, eyeing me over its flaming, stinger-laden tail.

I shrank back, but the creature only narrowed its eyes at me, then spun back toward the snakes and let out a horrifying snarl that sounded like a cross between an angry bobcat and the territorial alligator I'd heard hiss once on an animal show on TV.

The sound shot a shiver straight through me, but apparently it did the same to the snakes, because they flinched back, then nearly slithered over each other in their hurry to escape into the darkness.

The Void fell silent again, except for my shallow, panicked breathing, which suddenly felt *very* loud.

The creature's hackles lowered, its spine sank back into a normal stance, and it slowly turned around to face me.

Its face was completely feline, exactly like an ordinary house cat, except for having a face as large as a tiger's and tufted ears kind of like a bobcat — all made of flame. It tilted its head at me like a curious Husky, and I might have even thought the creature was cute had it not been probably capable of killing me in a millisecond. Then it sat on its haunches, and its flames wicked out.

The Void was suddenly in complete darkness again.

I sat, teeth clenched, praying the creature would take pity and not attack me, or at least decide to play with me before it ate me like cats sometimes do, so I'd have a chance to escape. As my eyes adjusted once again to the dark, the subtle glow of Callan's stone returned into focus, illuminating my hands.

I held the stone out, hand shaking, as I pushed slowly to my feet.

Two cat eyes glinted green, reflecting the stone's glow, nearly at eye level with me when I stood. The cat creature sat inches away, staring at me with its tilted head and curious gaze. It had fur now, or something like normal fur, from what I could see, all a ruddy brown color and with what looked like dark stripes. Its tail twitched in the air behind it, also furry except for the very scorpion-like stinger embedded on its end.

I shivered.

The creature lit with a gentle glow—nothing like the blazing brightness of before, this time more like a pinkish-yellow haze that reminded me of my Himalayan salt rock lamp at home—and stood, then flicked its head toward the right.

I gaped at it.

It stared at me, shook its fur out, and flicked its head again. Twice. While making intense eye contact. I swear it nearly rolled its eyes at me.

I swallowed. "You—you want me to *follow* you?"

The cat thing gave a subtle nod, then spun on its massive glowing paws and strode off in the direction it had nodded.

I stood for a moment, adjusting the heavy backpacks of supplies on my shoulders and debating my options. I could wait here in the dark and possibly get eaten, or I could try to find my way through the Void alone... and possibly get eaten. Or I could follow this flaming cat thing that just saved my life and... possibly get eaten. Of the three options, the cat creature was the only one that had, in fact, succeeded in *not* getting me eaten once already.

The glowing creature was already fading into the distant darkness, apparently no longer concerned about waiting for me.

I heaved a deep breath, said a quick prayer I wasn't about to die a horrific death, and hurried to catch up with the glowing cat-scorpion.

# CHAPTER 2

# WHY DID THEY EVEN LET ME HAVE THIS THING?

*Jordan*

If you'd told me a few days ago I'd be huddled in the dark trying to whisper sweet nothings to Madison Kane, I'd never have believed you. Of course, I also wouldn't have believed I'd be stuck in a cell in a Fae dungeon, or that those "sweet nothings" would be instructions on how to duck and cover because I was about to blow a hole in the prison wall. But here we were.

"Madison?"

I'd whispered to her several times since the guard left her in the cell across from mine. When she first arrived, she'd called my name and told me she and I were most likely being held as bait for Ayla, but a little while later, she'd gone mysteriously silent. I was starting to worry. "Madison!" Had she fallen asleep?

I shifted closer to the bars of my cell, straining to see her through the dark. No luck. It was black as death in here.

I tried once more, futilely, to light my flames, but whatever they warded these cells with was absolute. I could feel it, like a subtle static to the air. Probably a faespell to neutralize magic, or at least that had to be part of it, because my LeyGuard magic didn't work here. I'd tried a million times down here alone before Madison arrived. It made sense to ward against magic, for a prison most likely built to hold Fae. But it was still annoying.

How long had I even been here? It seemed like a day or two, maybe, but the darkness and silence made time stretch in strange ways. I leaned against the bars again.

"Madison."

Still nothing.

I stifled a curse and fingered the cold, flat metallic circle I'd pulled from my boot a few minutes earlier. It was a handy little thing, courtesy of Doctor Harlowe at the Hub—a runed coin stacked with three charges of LeyGuard wardspells that could counteract a variety of types of Fae magic for a brief period. Not that they handed such things out to LeyGuard trainees. I *may* have swiped it after Doctor Harlowe's technology rundown at the logistics meeting before my parents and Reina and I headed to the warehouse at the docks to do recon on Sevryn's operation. Only borrowed, of course. I'd planned to return it.

A cringe passed through me. I'd been reckless in the warehouse—but my team had gotten Ayla's parents and grandfather out. I'd seen that much. So it had been worth it.

Sevryn himself had been guarding Ayla's parents, but I hadn't seen the hidden Selkblood posse. I'd been face-to-face with Sevryn when several more Selkbloods flooded in and things went sideways. My parents and Reina were facing off against a couple of other Selkbloods while I tried to get past Sevryn, right before I was bashed in the head from behind and dragged through a breach. I woke up in this dungeon, and I hadn't seen anyone but the guards and Madison since I'd been here.

I hoped my parents and Reina were all okay.

According to Madison, Ayla and the others had been scouring Ayla's grandfather's journal, looking for a way to help the Fae prince and Ayla's parents—and to find and rescue *me*—when Madison was snatched by the Fadehound that brought her here. I should've known Ayla wouldn't sit back and let the LeyGuard handle everything; the anxiety of sitting still waiting for someone else to fix things would've driven her insane. But I'd sort of *hoped* she would let them handle it. Because then she'd be safe, and I could focus on gathering intel and getting myself—and now Madison—out of here smoothly.

*Ayla.* I'd be lying if I said replaying that parting kiss again and again in my mind wasn't the main thing that had kept me sane down here in this dungeon. But it also drove me a bit crazy. I was impatient to get back to her, to continue what we'd started. But what *had* we started? I still couldn't believe she'd said she finally wanted to be more than friends—but the darkness down here had given me a lot of time to worry that maybe I'd misunderstood her. Or that my impulsive declaration of intense feelings right before I ran off to a mission might have made her change her mind.

I couldn't believe I'd actually told her I *loved* her. I was an idiot. Not that it wasn't true. It absolutely was. But it probably also made her feel she needed to reciprocate, though I never expected her to. She tended to overthink things. Had I made her feel pressured? Just the thought of that set me on edge. I needed to talk to her, to explain—and to find out where we really stood.

But first, I needed to make sure she was *safe*. And it was hard to do that from a dungeon.

I'd half expected the Hub to send a team after me already. It was why I hadn't yet used the coin: I'd thought I might need it during our getaway. Mission protocol for captured trainees was to sit tight, gather intel, wait for extraction. But if Madison and I had both been brought here to lure Ayla out, as Madison suggested, then the Fae *knew* Ayla would be coming for us. I couldn't just sit around waiting to be rescued.

Madison might be a damsel in distress, but I wasn't. And I definitely wasn't going to be *bait*. I would not allow Ayla to risk her own life to save mine.

Wait. It suddenly struck me that Madison said she'd been dragged here by a *Fadehound*. Oh, no. There was only one way a Fadehound could carry a human—with its teeth. And Fadehound saliva was toxic. Madison's silence was suddenly a lot more alarming.

I scrambled to my feet and reached through the bars, but the walkway between our cells was too wide for me to reach anything. I tried a little louder, barely above a whisper. "Madison!" She answered me with a low moan.

Now I was definitely worried. If Madison had been bitten by a Fade-hound, she had a day or so, at best, before the toxin made its way to her heart or brain. Maybe less, depending on where she'd been bitten. "Madison!"

I clutched the coin. It only had three charges, but I needed to see how bad off Madison was. If I used one charge to neutralize the magic dampener on the cells, I could access my flame. My normal flame wouldn't burn through prison bars, but it did make light. And I'd still have two charges for the rest of my escape plan. With any luck, I'd only need one.

It wasn't a complicated plan—the guard who patrolled the cells carried an old-school sort of shotgun, the kind they packed with ammo and gunpowder in old Western movies. Apparently Fae hadn't advanced their weapons technology much, but then again, I supposed they hadn't needed to, the way the air ran thick with magic here. My guess was the ward that canceled out my magic also canceled out the guard's... and the gun was his backup protection. The door at the end of the hall seemed to seal shut behind him; he had to unlock it to let himself out every time he finished his rounds down here. I'd glimpsed the hall beyond that door, and it had at least one window — I'd seen it, all barred up, with a glimpse of sky outside.

So all I needed was to convince him to open my cell somehow, knock him out, grab his gun, neutralize the ward with my runed coin, grab his keys, stack his ammo and powder in the hall outside, set the powder off with my flames to blast a hole through the outer wall, and run like the wind.

It would work. Right? Or it *could* have—if Madison hadn't been wounded. Now, I wasn't sure. I hadn't planned on carrying an unconscious girl over my shoulder.

I groaned. Not for the first time, I missed Champ and Reina. Plans were always better with an armored dog and a partner to have your back. But at least they were safe. Madison had said they were at the cabin with the others when she was taken.

Right now, I needed to make sure Madison was okay.

I rubbed my thumb over the rune on the coin, then focused on the static buzz of the ward in my mind to target the rune's magic and spoke the word to activate it. The coin hummed warmly in my hand.

The static I'd felt since the moment I arrived fell away as the Fae ward disappeared. I huffed a sigh of relief. I hadn't realized how much that constant buzz was disorienting me until it vanished.

I jammed my arm between the bars toward Madison to call up my flame. Fire flared to life on my fingertips, tiny campfires casting mini glows.

I spun around my cell quickly, looking for something to ignite for a larger flame, but there was nothing. I pushed more power into my hand, letting the flames grow bigger.

I could sustain a flame like this for a little while—longer than most Valos House trainees at the Hub, actually—but I'd need food and water to replenish myself, sooner or later. Every Valos trainee reacted a bit differently to using their magic, based on their unique talents, but for me, using flame magic was like ramping my metabolism into overdrive.

I strained my arm as far as I could reach through the bars. There. I could barely make out Madison, sprawled out on her side on the stone floor.

"Madison!"

She didn't stir.

I dropped to my knees, hoping to get the flame a bit closer to her level.

She was pale in the flickering light, lips dry and cracked. Her hair was a mass of knots and leaves and dirt. Dark circles crested her eyes. How long ago had she been taken by the Fadehound? Had they brought her straight here? She was breathing—I could make out a subtle movement of her ribs. But beyond her shallow breaths, she was still as death.

I scooted down a few bars, taking in the rest of her.

There it was, the bite. Straight through her jeans above her left knee. It had dragged her here by her *thigh*? I winced. That had to have been unpleasant.

The bite mark was red and swollen, and I could see the edges of the wound through her torn jeans. Tendrils of purple were already spreading outward from it. The toxin moving through her veins.

My schedule for escape had just been accelerated.

My flames winked out. My heart pounded as I calculated how long the rune's effects had lasted. The ward had been disabled about a minute, maybe two? Not much time to pull off an escape. And I was working with only two remaining charges.

Thirst hit me as soon as my magic faded, but it was bearable. I'd worry about getting water once we were out of here.

I peeled off my jacket and shoved my sleeve up, then trailed my fingers to the etched rune on my bicep.

Chairman Hart had only allowed this tattoo as an emergency measure—technically trainees weren't even supposed to get them, but my parents had insisted I have a failsafe, in case... well, in case of something like this.

They'd made me promise to use it only if it was life or death. It was supposed to allow me to channel my flame into an inferno, or something like that. But I hadn't exactly been trained on how to wield it. Doctor Harlowe's distracted instructions had been less than helpful: "It's like an emergency flotation device. You just yank the cord and figure it out. But whatever you do, don't yank it until you need it. And for heaven's sake, make sure there are no explosives around."

*Yanking the cord* was not as clear as I'd have hoped, given that the symbol tattooed on my arm had no cords to yank. But I'd gathered the meaning of his metaphor—pull it out, let 'er rip, and hope for the best.

It wasn't the first time I'd wondered if the "Safety Regulations" manual I'd seen hanging on Doctor Harlowe's wall was actually just a bunch of blank papers, and I was sure it wouldn't be the last.

He'd taught me the name of the rune, which wasn't necessary for most LeyGuards to activate one, but he'd said speaking it might help me channel it. That would have to be enough.

I tied my leather jacket around my waist—not my favorite look but it *was* my favorite jacket and I wasn't about to leave it behind in a Fae dungeon for some cold-hearted Selkblood to wear—and stepped back from the bars, since Madison would never forgive me if I singed her eyebrows off.

Who knew what I was about to create with this thing, but if nothing else, it should cause a bit of a distraction.

I clutched the runed coin once more, said a quick prayer I wasn't about to spontaneously combust myself, then turned toward the outer door.

"Hey!" I yelled at the top of my lungs. "Hey! We need help in here!"

I counted out the time in my head. Thirty seconds. A minute. No one came.

I sighed, then sucked in a deep breath and yelled again. "Hey! Hey! A prisoner's escaping!"

That one got the guard's attention. I heard scuffling. I hated lying under any circumstances, but it was technically true—I was actively attempting to escape. I hoped God would forgive the slight deception.

There was a clang, and the door swung in. Light spilled in from the hall outside.

Our usual guard tromped down the three stone steps from the door to the walkway, carrying a lantern that gave off only a faint flickering glow, his usual light source when he didn't want to "waste power" searing my eyeballs from the fluorescents above after so long in the dark. I'd gathered that electricity was rationed in Teionyr, or maybe only in its prisons.

The guard stormed toward us and swept his eyes over us both—we clearly weren't escaping yet—then groaned in frustration and glared at me. "Stop yelling. You'll disturb the—"

"Please." I decided to try a peaceful tactic first. I had no desire to harm him if I didn't have to. He might have a family. "My friend needs help. She's been bitten."

The guard held out his lantern toward Madison. Her wound was evident, but he just shrugged. "Not my problem."

I narrowed my eyes at him. "It is if you want her as bait."

He sneered at me. "Not all bait needs to be alive."

"So you'll just let her die?" Fury flared in my chest.

He shrugged. "What's it to me? I get paid, either way."

I eyed him. He didn't look like a Selkblood, but he also didn't look Teionyrian. Was he a mercenary? "Who do you work for?"

He laughed. "Same as everyone in Teionyr these days. King Beirthyr and Lord Sevryn."

"King Beirthyr and *Lord* Sevryn?" I probed. He'd said that like Sevryn was almost the king's equal. That was unsettling.

The guard grunted. "Lord Sevryn is the king's right hand. We *all* serve at his pleasure, these days, by the king's command." He sneered at me. "Even you."

He was talking. I could work this. I clutched the bars. "Why use us as bait, anyway? What's he after?"

His grin twisted into a scowl. "You ask too many questions, *guardblood*." He spat the last word like it was a curse, then turned for the steps. "Call me if she dies. We'll want to get her out before she stinks." He yanked the outer door open.

*Perfect.*

"Hey!" I called toward his back. "Do you have a family? Like... kids? A wife? Anyone you go home to at night?"

He laughed, still holding the door ajar. "Not unless pub wenches count."

That was all I needed to know. I whispered the word to activate the coin, then pressed my fingers to the tattoo the moment I felt the static fall away. "*Igni.*"

My arm exploded with a torrent of flame. Like a flamethrower. Coming from my *bicep*.

"What the—!" I heard the guard yell, though the rest of his words fell away.

I was too busy trying to wield the geyser of flame that had melted straight through my cell bars to hear whatever else he said.

"Gah!" I spun away from my cell door to keep the flames from roasting Madison and climbed backward through the hole left by the molten metal.

A drop of it hit my boot and sizzled.

I kicked the drop off just as the guard rushed me.

He lunged to tackle me, but as I jumped back, my flame swept over him.

He reeled back, howling, knocked his head against a cell bar, and sank to the floor.

I stared at my arm. This was *way* more dangerous than a flotation device. "Why did they even let me *have* this thing?!"

I rushed toward Madison's cell, trying my best to focus the flame into one spot on her cell bars.

It melted through the metal in an instant, and I ran another sweep closer to the ground, then the section of bars clanged to the floor, forming a makeshift door.

I tried to focus on the rune to reel the magic in so I could reach Madison safely, but it seemed to have gone haywire. My whole arm was like a wall of spewing flame.

Now I *knew* Doctor Harlowe's safety manual was a sham.

A curtain of static swept over me suddenly, and the flame winked out as the prison ward snapped back into place.

I sucked a couple wheezing breaths and surveyed the damage.

Patches of my flame still smoldered where it had ignited the oil spilled from the guard's broken lantern. The guard himself was out cold on the floor, a safe distance from the burning oil. His hair was singed, but it looked like he was breathing—at least I hadn't killed him. The door to the hall still hung ajar, just barely.

Relief swept over me. I wouldn't have to risk waking the guard to dig for his keys.

"I am *never* doing that again," I muttered, then rushed toward Madison. "Come on, we have to get out of here."

She hung limp over my shoulder as I hauled her up, sending a wave of concern through me. But she did moan when I pressed my arms around her thighs to steady her weight.

"Sorry," I whispered. The bite area probably hurt like a beast.

I never imagined I'd be breaking out of a Fae dungeon with Madison Kane slung over my shoulder, but I hadn't imagined a *lot* of things about this experience.

I steadied my grip on her and ran for the door.

I fingered the coin in my palm as I reached the stairs—one charge left—and took the first two steps in one stride. My boots hit the top landing. I yanked open the outer door.

"Where do you think you're going?" a voice snapped.

A tall, pale figure stood on the other side of the door, blocking our exit. *Sevryn.*

# Chapter 3

# Last Chance for Second Thoughts

***Striker***

The last Shadowhound burst to ash in my arms and I stepped back, finally dropping my flame. My skin felt dry—that dehydrated sunburned feel—but that was nothing unusual.

I glanced around. I'd taken a dozen of them, alone. Maybe more. A grin tugged at my lips. Brone would be irked. His record was eleven.

I winced as my gaze swept over the trees and foliage. The forest behind Maddox Rogers' cabin had seen better days. The back wall of the cabin now sported a new charred aesthetic, and every tree and shrub in a ten-foot radius was seared to a crisp.

I hadn't meant to damage so much of the area, but some straggler hounds had tried to breach in after Ayla while I was tied up with three others, and I'd sent out a heat blast to stop them. Mission accomplished. Not a thing had made it through that breach but the girl. If there were any cute little bunnies in these woods, though, hopefully they'd high-tailed it before things got crispy.

Maddox would forgive me about the charred wall, I knew—not that he ever came out here anymore. He might not even remember it existed. I supposed the cabin fell to Ayla now, but it wasn't like she would hold it against me. I'd saved her from the hounds.

I could only hope nothing worse had gotten her since she'd been in the Veil.

The Hub would start asking questions about Ayla and Reina's whereabouts, sooner or later, but hopefully I could find Ayla and her friends and get them back Earthside before the Hub realized what had happened.

Besides, I had my own investigating to do. Dark Fae breaching Earthside through woods protected by Hub-controlled wards was no accident. Until I figured out who might be responsible for this, it was best if word about the cabin and what had happened out here spread as little as possible.

I dusted Shadowhound ash off my hands onto my pants, then pulled a new match out from my matchbook to replace the one the buggers had knocked out of my mouth. If I didn't have a stomach of steel, the stench of burnt Shadowhound would've been enough to make me gag. But you see things, as a LeyGuard. It doesn't take long to break you or bake you... harden you, like pottery in a kiln. You could still be broken later, though. Some things, no one should see.

In my case, I'd forged a stomach of steel, but I'd worked hard to keep my heart from following suit. Hard hearts in hard men only created victims; I'd seen it a hundred times too many. Not that I didn't *act* like a cold brute. That act had its uses. But my bleeding heart got me in trouble more times than I could count—like right now, standing in the woods, about to commit an unauthorized breach into the Veil just to ensure some teenager wouldn't get murdered. The Hub would have my head for this... if they ever found out. But I intended to keep my head, in every sense of the term.

I slid my phone out. Brone was back at the Hub, waiting for me to check in.

*How's it looking there?* I texted him.

As my LeyGuard partner of more than fifteen years, Brone was the only one who knew about my secret, gooey center. He'd been with me Faeside during the early years of the Dark Fae war, when we pulled Faeblood children from the rubble—nothing had ever seared my flames hot and broken me all at once like that did. The stuff we'd faced together, that was brotherhood, if ever there was one. And as a marksman and ore wielder, Brone was without equal. It didn't matter that he was Ordas House and I was Valos; there had never been a House rivalry with us, nothing to prove. He was my brother, and there was no one I trusted more.

Right now, Brone was also the *only* person I truly trusted at the Hub. Chairman Hart and the others weren't acting right. I hadn't figured out why, yet, but if my gut was correct—and it usually was—it had something to do with Ayla and this breach.

*Hart's on a rampage, but I've got it under control,* Brone texted back.

I winced at that. I'd hoped it might take Chairman Hart a bit longer to notice my absence, though I doubted she'd yet connected it with Ayla's.

I kept telling myself it was the lingering mystery about the breaches, not my sorry bleeding heart, that ended me out here in the woods about to commit a Class 5 LeyGuard infraction. Either way, I'd made the girl a promise, and I intended to keep it. I was going after her. But that didn't mean I wanted to leave Maddox Rogers unattended. That old man knew more than even *he* realized, and something about his and Ayla's situation with the Hub still wasn't adding up.

*Watch the old man,* I texted Brone. *Going breach.*

*On it,* he texted back.

His next text came through a moment later: *Godspeed.*

We both knew there was no point in telling each other to be careful. We would each do what needed to be done—and if we were lucky, we might even survive it. If not, well, with my power I could *literally* go out in a flame of glory. I supposed I couldn't ask for a better end than that.

I pocketed my phone and turned toward the buzzing section of air near the treeline—the activated Leyline. I *hated* going Faeside. I could feel the Fae magic on every inch of me when I was there, like tiny gnats burrowing into my pores. Every LeyGuard felt it differently, but for me that's how it was. And this part of the Veil was even worse—a Void full of creatures seeping dark magic, which for me meant the added bonus of a rotten-berries taste on the back of my tongue. Fun. I reached my hand out toward the breach.

The air shimmered and heated as my LeyGuard runes activated. The breach split open, a shimmering rip in the air with only darkness visible beyond. A shiver rushed over me at the thought of all that Fae magic. Now was my last chance for second thoughts, but since right now the Veil held a teenage girl I'd promised to protect, imaginary skin-gnats and rancid berries it was. I sighed and stepped through into the darkness.

As soon as the breach snapped shut behind me, I swiped my match over the patch of sandpaper on my cross-belt and used its heat to light a small flame in each hand. The match wasn't necessary to activate my magic, strictly speaking, but I liked the boost it gave, kind of like downing an energy shot. The Fae magic was already itching my skin, and I was slightly disappointed when my fire revealed nothing killable in the immediate vicinity. It would've been a good distraction. I supposed I'd make better time finding Ayla this way, though. Slaughtering tended to delay one's itinerary. Maybe there'd be something good to kill when I located her.

I slid a runestone from my pocket—a locator tied to the one I'd given Ayla. Theoretically, its rune would pick up her stone's signature and cast a beam of light to lead me right to her. But I couldn't say I was shocked when the rune on its surface simply flickered then died. Runespells seldom went as planned in the Veil. Too much dark magic interfering. I'd have to find her the old-fashioned way: by looking.

If I used the runestone as a weak antenna, I should be able to decipher from its flickers whether I was heading the right way, like a game of hot and cold. Or I could make a ruckus and draw out a lesser dark Fae to force information out of. The latter seemed more fun.

I planted my feet on the flat expanse of darkness—never had gotten used to that weirdness—and shot my flames out high. "Hey! Voidspawn! Come and get me!"

It only took a few seconds for the first monsters to bite—literally. But Void-snakes were easy pickings if you had flames, and they never got close enough to close their fangs on anything more than the hardened leather of my boot. I kicked their charred bodies aside. Couldn't question a snake.

I needed something verbal: a Veil-Dearg, a redcap, I wasn't picky. I'd even take a darkened leprechaun, though they gave me the creeps. Big talkers, though. I could use that.

I pushed more magic into my flames, until they danced like blazing columns from each fist, casting wild shadows that melted back into the darkness. No Void-Fae within a mile would fail to see that. There was bound to be *something* nearby worth questioning. Here in the Veil, though, you heard things before you saw them, especially when *you* were the light source. I strained my ears, listening over the crackle of my flames.

In the distance, something screamed.

I froze.

The scream had sounded *human*.

It wasn't a girl's scream, so not Ayla. It had been a male's, something between a yell of pain and a frightened pansy-boy shriek. It could be a trick, but it could also be one of Ayla's missing friends.

The scream was followed by loud thumping.

I doused my flames and ran in that direction.

The landscape was bizarre in the Void, an abyss of nothing-darkness until suddenly you crashed into a Void tree or toppled headlong off a ledge into a cursed pond or something. I slowed, not eager to smash my face into an invisible boulder or take a sudden dunk with baby Fae-krakens, and waited for my eyes to adjust to the lack of flames.

Once my eyes adapted to the dark again, it didn't take long to spot the source of the thumping. Some huge reptile monstrosity was throwing a tantrum, clomping its giant feet at the mouth of a Void-cave. It looked sort of like a stegosaurus, but it was far more hideous than any dinosaur I'd ever seen in my grade-school textbooks. It was like someone had taken a dinosaur, boiled most of its skin off, then dipped it in a pit of tar. This was a new one, even for the LeyGuard manuals.

A shudder raced through me. New Voidspawn meant the Dark Fae had been busy. That was never good news.

The stego-thing screeched like a raptor and reared back, raising up on its hind legs to slam its massive forefeet down on the cave's stony entrance. The stone let out a loud crack, and the creature reared up again. That in itself defied physics; the creature's body shape didn't look as though it should move that way. But I wasn't about to stand around debating its exercise routines; whoever was in that cave was in trouble.

The runes on my arm surged with a hum as my flames rushed through me. It was a heady feeling, almost enough to chase the gnats away, though it did nothing about the rancid air-taste. I channeled the full force of my magic into a flaming whip—showy, but effective. Especially when you needed to lasso a stego-thing before it slammed its big, fat feet into a cave again.

"Hey! Ugly!"

The creature halted partway through raising its forefeet and flicked its head around to look at me.

*Lands alive*, this thing was hideous. Strips of skin hung around its bony eye sockets, and its mouth was like a turtle's, but with fangs.

It lowered its forefeet and turned slowly around to face me.

How could this thing even *see* without eyes? But maybe it hunted some other way, like smell.

If that was the case, I was offering a feast—nothing stank quite like LeyGuard sweat mixed with flame smoke and charred Shadowhound.

It fixed its empty eye sockets on me.

"Come and get me!" I yelled again.

It stamped the ground like a bull, then charged toward me.

I smiled and swung my whip.

Just before my flame slashed into its target, I shaped the end into a lasso and snapped it tight, snagging the beast's massive neck and shoulders.

The stego shrieked, but kept charging.

I fed power into the flames, searing the beast's flesh. The stench was immediate and awful—worse than the Shadowhounds—but the beast kept coming.

"Huh." I stared at it a moment. Heat resistant skin? I'd expected it to crumple to ash with the heat surge, like most other Fae beasts. I supposed I should run.

I spun, leaving my searing whip behind to annoy the beast, and conjured up two columns of flame, tossing them behind me to gain me some distance. The beast barrelled right *through* them instead of dodging around them, which hampered that strategy a bit.

"Well. *Voids.*" My flames weren't cutting it. I needed a new tactic.

I spun back toward the beast and flung myself onto its face. My arms weren't long enough to fully restrain its massive fang-beak. It snapped at me, and I barely evaded limb-loss in time to vault my legs up over its neck. Suddenly I was riding the thing. Not exactly my plan, but it would do.

The beast skidded to a stop and reared, seeming startled at this turn of events.

*You and me both, buddy.* But now what? I clung with both arms and legs to one of the thing's bony spine-plates as it attempted to fling me off. But this wasn't my first rodeo—literally. It would take more than a temper tantrum to buck me off a bull, even one this ugly. The problem would be figuring out what to do from here. Its whole back was ridged with bone. If I could work my dagger loose, I could go for the underside of its throat; it seemed more penetrable. But I'd need to distract it long enough to swing around and get the right angle. Could I jam my fingers into its eye sockets? Were they even sensitive? My flame-lasso still sizzled around the creature's shoulders, casting a faint light but doing little else. I slid my dagger free from my belt with one hand, evaluating my options.

Something metallic flew toward me, glinting in my flames, and buried itself in the creature's throat.

"Voids!"

The beast shrieked and reared again, and I took the opportunity to drive my own dagger into its throat beside the one that had nearly taken off my hand.

The beast staggered, swayed. And fell.

I dove off and tumbled, then sprang to my feet just in time to see it hit the ground. It burst up in a huge rush of flame.

*Huh.* Apparently its flame-resistance only worked while it was alive, some sort of inherent warding. Interesting.

I strode forward and extracted both daggers from the stream of my own residual flame, and wiped them off on my pants. "Ugh. Stego guts."

"I don't suppose I could have that back, now?"

I glanced up to find familiar eyes watching me. My lips pulled up into a grin. "Callan. I should've known that was a Fae throw. No one but a Fae or Ordas-born can steer a blade like that." I handed him his weapon. "You nearly severed my hand off, though. You might need to work on your aim, after all."

Callan smirked. "Ridiculous. I never miss." His smile vanished. "I need your help."

He jogged toward the cave and I followed, wondering how a skilled Fae guard like Callan had managed to let a Void beast trap him in a cave.

"Some light, please?" Callan asked.

As soon as I lit my flames, I understood. He hadn't been cornered; he'd been protecting someone. A very badly injured someone, lying in a pool of way too much blood.

*Rory Kane.*

# CHAPTER 4

# WHATEVER YOU NEED

*Ayla*

The scorpion-cat didn't turn back to wait for me, but it did slow its pace, allowing me to catch up. I followed a few steps behind it, safely out of reach of its swishing stinger-tail. The silence of the Void settled down over us, punctuated by the clumsy thump of my steps. I tried to roll my feet as I walked to quiet them.

Somehow, the cat walked in complete silence, despite its massive paws.

I watched it warily as we walked. A glowing scorpion-cat didn't seem to be the kind of creature you should trust blindly—not that I was ungrateful it had saved me. But *why* had it saved me? And where was it taking me?

The stone beneath my shirt surged brighter, suddenly, and a fresh wave of warm fuzzies washed through me. I gasped and stared at the cat. Could it be... "Kaizyn?"

The cat glanced at me over its shoulder with definitively judgy side-eye, then huffed and turned forward again.

Was that an annoyed *no*? Or an annoyed *yes*? Or was it just telling me to be quiet? Scorpion-cats should come with a body language interpretation guide or something. I shifted the backpack straps—they were digging into my shoulders again—and continued following it in silence.

The stone surged again, a burst of light and warmth, then I felt a *yank* on my heart much stronger than before. *This way, hurry!*

The cat must've felt it too, because its tufted ears perked, and it glanced back for only a second, then burst into motion.

"Wait! Where are you going?" I raced after the cat as quickly as I could with two bulky backpacks bouncing against me, but it was rapidly leaving me behind. I huffed, already out of breath. "Wait!"

The cat turned to the right and disappeared, like it'd turned a corner or something, but there *were* no corners here. There was *nothing here*, just a bunch of empty, black—

*Oof.* I smashed headlong into something and toppled back onto my rear.

I grunted and heaved myself up—which wasn't easy with two backpacks to juggle—and rubbed my sore face. Nothing seemed broken, but I might have some bruising on my nose. At the moment, though, I could hardly bring myself to care—the stone was sending out pulses of warm fuzzies so strong it nearly felt like a drug. *Good heavens.* I could only assume that meant I was heading the right direction. I carefully extracted the glowing stone from my chest and held it out, using its light to see what I'd smashed into.

It looked... like a tree. Or at least what a tree might look like if it was completely black. Black bark, black branches sprawling out overhead, and from what I could see of the rest above, clusters of thin, black leaves. There was even black grass around the base of the tree. *Weird.* The trunk itself was about my arm span in width, and I couldn't see much past it. But I remembered the cat had turned right...

I edged clockwise around to the back of the tree, then pointed myself in the direction the cat's right-hand turn would've taken it. There was nothing back here. Other than the tree, the stone's glow showed nothing else in the area at all. The cat had abandoned me.

A feral shriek sliced the Void, followed by a loud thunk.

The warm-fuzzy pulses from the stone vanished suddenly and its glow winked out, plunging me into utter darkness.

I forced deep breaths, barely keeping a grip on my panic. *Okay. What now?*

The stone's glow surged back to life in my hand just as I heard an unfamiliar voice shout—

"Ayla! Watch out!"

Something slammed into me from behind.

The weight of the backpacks swung forward, and I toppled, unable to catch myself as I crashed into the hard ground. One foot twisted at a bad angle as I fell.

I yanked my arms from the backpack straps and flipped over onto my back, ready to fight for my life.

The cat-scorpion stared down at me, full flaming again, like when I'd first seen it.

I gaped up at it as I shoved awkwardly to my feet. "*Ouch.*" I'd definitely bruised up my knees and shins and elbows and maybe even my ribs in the fall. I could move everything, nothing was broken, but I felt like—well, like I'd belly-flopped onto hard ground, which I basically *had*. I put my weight fully on my legs, and let out a hiss of pain. One ankle was definitely sprained. I could probably manage to walk on it, but it was going to hurt. I glared at the scorpion-cat. "Why did you *do* that?"

It huffed, but before it could roll its eyes at me again, a figure darted toward us from the darkness.

"Ayla! Are you okay?"

I froze. Deep blue eyes stared back at me from the edge of the cat's orange glow. Tannish skin. Dark brown hair that fell haphazardly over one side of his forehead. That perfect face.

"*Kaizyn.*" He was still utterly handsome, though I found that it was purely a surface reaction, now, like acknowledging a stunning sunset or impressive storm. He was eye-catching... but there were no flutters in my chest from it. My heart belonged to someone else.

Kaizyn hurried toward me. "I felt your fear... and then your pain. Are you hurt?"

I gaped at him far longer than was socially acceptable, then muttered, "Yeah. I'm fine."

I suddenly realized I'd just called a prince I'd never officially met by his *first name*. Didn't they *behead* people in some places for an offense like that?

"I'm sorry," I said quickly. "A moment ago, I meant, *Prince* Kaizyn? Or... Your Highness?" I felt my face flush and knew I must be beet-red. "I didn't mean to offend."

He shook his head quickly, his eyes still studying me with concern. "No, please. We are... bonded. Kaizyn is fine."

What was I supposed to say to *that*?

Kaizyn drew a little breath and took a step back, seeming uncertain, then glanced away and ran his hand through his messy brown hair. He turned back toward me, dropped his hand and shoved it in his pocket. "Now *I* must apologize. I shouldn't have brought up the bond. I know you didn't choose it—and I owe you my life. I swear to you, I will do everything in my power to remove it as soon as possible, so long as that's still what you wish."

I stared blankly at him, then nodded. "Yes... please." I didn't mean to offend him, but despite jumping through a portal into this hellish place, betrothal to a cursed Fae prince was *not* something I'd signed up for.

He sucked in a quick breath. "Then that is what we will do." He glanced around suddenly, seeming puzzled. "Where's Callan? Isn't he with you?"

I blinked at him. "No. He ran off, after Madison."

Kaizyn's eyes widened. "He sent you in here *alone*?"

"No. I mean, yes... kind of. He gave me the stone, but I didn't *mean* to come alone, Striker was supposed to—" I stopped, realizing none of that would make sense without more context. "Let me start over. Yes, he sent me alone. But only because he was trying to save someone else. He said the stone would bring me to you." I paused, studying his face. "I—I need your help."

Kaizyn nodded. "Of course. Whatever you need. I will help in any way I can."

I sighed in relief. "Thank you. I—Wait, why are you wearing *jeans*?"

Those weren't the words I *meant* to expel from my mouth, but it had just occurred to me that he was wearing normal clothes, instead of the Ren-Faire type ones I'd first seen him in. He was wearing jeans, Converse, and a Henley shirt—which, when I looked more closely at it, sent a wave of sorrow and longing through me at how much it looked like something Jordan would wear.

Kaizyn took another step backward. "I'm sorry. Is it... wrong? I asked Callan to bring me some Earthside clothes to wear, so that the next time I breached to see you, you might feel more comfortab—I'm sorry. I shouldn't have, that was presumptuous. I can change, when we..."

He seemed so anxious he was giving *me* anxiety. I shook my head quickly. "No, no, it's fine. I just wasn't expecting it."

He stopped rambling as his gaze swept over me again.

He still looked so uncomfortable, I felt a surge of sympathy for him. "They look good on you, actually." The words came out small, though they were true.

Kaizyn watched me for a long moment, then flinched. "You're hurt. I can still feel it." His hand twitched, almost like he was about to reach out to me, then clenched into a fist at his side. "Where are you injured? Can you walk? We need to get to safety."

"Safety? Why? What's—"

The scorpion-cat grunted and rolled its eyes at me again, and only *then* did I notice the giant, decapitated lizard-thing lying on its side in the dark behind where Kaizyn stood, and the sheathed sword hanging at Kaizyn's side.

"There will be more coming," Kaizyn said, following my gaze. "They don't venture far from their packs."

*Oh.* "You... I mean... I didn't..." *What was it about the Veil that muddled up all my thoughts and words?* I forced a deep breath and attempted to act like I still had brain cells. "Thank you. I'm guessing you and this grumpy scorpion-cat thing just saved my life."

Kaizyn laughed—a brilliant, pure sound that took me by surprise—and his deep blue eyes settled on mine again. He studied me for a long moment, and when he spoke again, it seemed like he was choosing his words carefully. "Perhaps, but seeing as we're bonded, I was only saving myself, no?" He stepped forward and cautiously held out a hand. "Can I help support you while we walk? I can tell you're still in pain." He gestured toward the cat. "Vyrthil can carry your bags."

I stared at the cat, who was glaring at me again. "You mean *him*? I'm pretty sure he hates me."

Kaizyn laughed again, and it did strange things to my chest. Not *romantic* things, exactly—I still cared only for Jordan, in that sense—but Kaizyn was... endearing. There was no other way to explain it. He felt like someone I could see as a close friend. Which was strange, because I barely knew him... and vibing with people instantly didn't usually happen to me. *Huh.* It was probably the bond.

Kaizyn shook his head. "Hate you? No." He cut his gaze to Vyrthil, then his eyes locked back on mine, this time with a sparkle of amusement. "He's just a grump, as you said."

Vyrthil grunted in what I could only assume was annoyance.

Kaizyn ignored him and gave me a warm smile. "No one could hate you." He reached out his hand. "Can I help you walk? Please. I don't want you to strain your injury more than necessary."

I eyed his hand for a moment, but my ankle *did* hurt, and something deep inside me told me I could trust him. My mind also cautioned me to be careful, but more for Kaizyn's sake than mine. I hadn't forgotten Callan's warning that Kaizyn felt a deep bond to me... and that he could also feel my emotions.

I pulled back as that sank in. Was that why he was acting so weird? I felt suddenly exposed. He was basically reading my mind.

Kaizyn's gaze softened. "You're afraid. I won't hurt you, Ayla. And you don't have to worry about hurting me. The bond—" He took a breath. "I wish I could change it, but I can't. I will do my best not to read you, but sometimes your emotions are so strong, they come through anyway—it's almost like I'm feeling them myself."

I studied him. His eyes were entirely sincere.

I sighed, then nodded. "Okay. And yes, I... could use a little help walking." I reached for his hand.

Kaizyn relaxed and smiled as his fingers closed around mine. "It would be my pleasure. Let's get you somewhere safe."

His hand was warmer than I expected, but I was even *more* surprised when I looked down and saw that his fingers were gently glowing, like Vyrthil's body had earlier.

Kaizyn followed my gaze as he stepped closer. "Oh. I'm sorry, I should've warned you. Teionyr is a fire-Fae kingdom. Our magic—well, it's different for every royal, I suppose, and mine isn't as strong as most..." He trailed off a little, seeming embarrassed, then recovered and lifted my arm over his shoulder so he could support me as we walked. "Anyway, when I've recently used my magic, it can leave a glow. But it's harmless. Just a residue."

"And Vyrthil is part of your magic, too? Or"—I glanced at the giant cat thing—"like a pet?"

Vyrthil huffed at the same time Kaizyn laughed. "No, neither," Kaizyn said. "Vyrthil is my sear-bind." He adjusted my arm. "Are you comfortable? Able to walk?"

I tested a step with Kaizyn's support, then nodded. "Yes, this is fine."

"Good." He smiled at me again, then gestured at Vyrthil, who scooped the straps of both backpacks up with his mouth and lifted them both like they weighed nothing.

We began walking slowly, though I had no clue toward what, since to me everything just looked like darkness.

While we walked, Kaizyn continued. "A sear-bind is a rite of passage for a Teionyrian royal—a ritual taught only by royal *to* royal, from one sitting king to the next in line for the throne when we come of age. Then we are taken to the Wilds..."

The way he said "Wilds" evoked thoughts of the fire swamp from *The Princess Bride*, which made me think of Jordan again, which shot a pang of worry and longing straight through my chest.

Kaizyn stumbled, glanced at me, then quickly averted his eyes. "I'm sorry. Are you all right?"

So he had felt *that,* too. As if it wasn't already awkward enough to walk with my arm around some guy I barely knew, leaning my weight into his side with every step. I forced back the mix of exasperated sigh and hot tears pressing at my throat, and nodded. "Yes, I'm fine."

Kaizyn glanced at me again, but to his credit, he just nodded and acted like nothing was strange. "Anyway, we do the ceremony there, in the Wilds, and—if we are worthy—a creature responds to our call and bonds to us. The power of the creature represents the strength of our magic."

I glanced back at Vyrthil. "Wow. You must be powerful."

Kaizyn laughed, but it was sad this time. "No—I am actually not. I am... average at best."

I couldn't help but look back at Vyrthil again. "Are you sure?"

When I turned back to look up at Kaizyn, his smirk looked amused. "Yes. I think I would know." He laughed softly again. "Don't get me wrong, I am quite fond of Vyrthil. He's an excellent sear-bind."

Somewhere behind us, Vyrthil chuffed.

"But for a royal..." Kaizyn sighed. "A fire-cat is a fairly common animal in the Wilds, even if not in the rest of Upper Faeside. To sear-bind with one is a sign of average magical strength, at best."

"Oh." I glanced up at him. I wasn't sure what else to say.

He shrugged. "It was quite the disappointment to my father, actually. He summoned a fire-gryphon, himself. Very rare. He was hoping I would summon something all the *more* impressive, something to assure our people that the throne remained secure, that their future king would be even stronger than their current king, able to protect his people in the burgeoning war." He shrugged again. "Instead, they got only me. And now..." His expression swept to anger.

"Now your uncle has betrayed you both, lied to your people, and stolen the throne."

"Yes." He sighed, then shook his head, and the anger seemed to melt away. "And I fear I am not strong enough to take it back."

When I glanced up at him again, his face held such despair, my heart couldn't help but go out to him. "I'll help you," I said suddenly. "If you can help me find my friends, we *all* will. We'll figure out this curse, get you unstuck from the Veil, and help you take back your kingdom." It was a lot to promise, but it was nothing Callan and Jordan and I and the others hadn't already discussed doing.

Kaizyn stopped walking and turned to face me. "You actually *mean* that, don't you?"

I met his stare. "Yes."

He studied me, then nodded. "You are a wonder, Ayla Rogers." Then he reached behind him and grabbed at part of the air—and it peeled right back in his hand, like a curtain.

I gasped. On closer inspection, it *was* a curtain, covering the opening to something. It blended in so well with the darkness, I hadn't seen it.

Kaizyn flicked his wrist, and a flaming orb shot out into the opening behind the curtain and hovered, lighting it up like a floating campfire. From the stone walls and arched ceiling the light revealed, the curtained opening seemed to be the mouth of a cave.

Kaizyn swept his arm toward the entrance. "Welcome to my lodgings."

The way he said it struck me as funny, and I laughed before I could stop myself. "Your *lodgings*?"

He blinked at me. "Is that not the right word? My tutors have long insisted I am fluent in your language, yet it seems I have much still to learn. This is my... place I remain safe, while in the Veil."

I felt embarrassed, suddenly, for laughing. All the stress was addling my brain. "No, it was right," I said quickly. "I just expected you to call it something else... like a hideout? A base camp? A refuge? I don't know, really, it just struck me as funny that you called it 'lodgings,' as if the prince of Teionyr just... lives in a cave."

Now *I* was the one rambling, and those deep blue, perceptive eyes weren't doing much good for clearing my brain. He was still reading me like a book, though I could tell he was trying not to.

One corner of his mouth quirked up into a smirk. "Should a prince *not* live in a cave?" He laughed softly. "It seems this one does. At least for now."

My spirits sank as I realized what this must all be like for him. "I'm sorry. I shouldn't have said that."

His intense blue eyes locked on mine. "Do not ever feel the need to apologize for your thoughts, Ayla Rogers." He smiled kindly, then swept the curtain open wider. "Now, let's get you inside and fix that ankle."

# CHAPTER 5

# MAN OF MY WORD

**_Jordan_**

"Y ou singed my guard and nearly escaped my prison, despite its wards," Sevryn said, scowling.

Even though the filtered sun from the barred window was at his back, his eyes glowed an unnatural shade of blue—the eyes of a Selkblood.

He crossed his arms and glared at me. "Explain to me why I shouldn't just kill you."

I shifted Madison's weight on my shoulder. She probably only weighed 120 pounds, but she was limp as a sack of flour and her hip bone was digging into my clavicle. I shrugged my free shoulder. "I could ask you the same."

Sevryn's icy eyes narrowed, evaluating my bluff, then he laughed. "If you could, you would've done it at the warehouse."

I met his stare. "I had other priorities." _Like getting Ayla's family out safely._ And I had succeeded—or I'd made it possible for my team to succeed, anyway. Ayla's parents and grandfather were safe. But Sevryn and I had unfinished business. Besides, if he'd wanted me dead, I wouldn't be standing here.

Sevryn studied me a moment longer, then waved a dismissive hand. "You're in _my_ domain, now... or have you not realized? I control this prison. I'm second in command of this entire _palace_. Whatever you have planned to escape, it won't work. You may as well surrender. I might even find a use for you, if you're cooperative." His hands clenched into fists at his side, betraying his anger. He really did *want* to kill me. So why was he holding back?

I was powerful, when I could access my magic, but Sevryn was one of the most powerful Selkbloods the Hub had ever encountered. Fae magic radiated off of him even through the prison's dampening wards, like it was struggling to burst free. And what he'd done to Madison's bodyguard wasn't even the half of it. As a Selkblood, Sevryn could manipulate emotions and perception. He could slip inside my head and convince me to hand Madison right over to him, if he wanted, or make me walk myself back into my cell and lock myself back in before I realized what I was doing. But he hadn't. He was toying with me. My question was *Why?*

"Besides, it would be a shame to kill the blonde," he added, then cut a creepy smile at Madison that sent a chill down my back.

I tightened my grip on Madison's legs. "Leave her alone."

He cut his eyes back to me with a threatening smirk. "And if I don't?"

Fury flared in my chest again, and I locked my eyes on his. I wasn't one for empty threats, and as much as I hated to admit it, I *was* on his turf. My magic would work for only a minute or two inside these walls if I activated the coin's last charge to disable the warding, but disabling the ward would free all of Sevryn's magic, too.

Right now, Sevryn seemed content to flaunt that he had the upper hand. But if I antagonized him into actually using his magic on me, he'd have me paralyzed with mind-games while he ripped out both our throats with his teeth, all in a matter of seconds. There'd be no way I could protect Madison and fend him off at the same time. So I had to be smart about this. He wanted to play? I would play. For now. But we would play by *my* rules.

I subtly slipped the rune-coin with its final charge into my pocket as I shifted Madison again. To my relief, Sevryn didn't seem to notice. It was vital that he not realize I had that coin. I might not be able to use it right now, but it was still my ticket out of here.

If I knew anything about Selkbloods like Sevryn—not *all* Selkbloods, of course, just the power-hungry types like him—they *loved* to know they had all the leverage in a situation. It had shown true with the group I'd encountered at the warehouse, and Sevryn seemed to be especially fond of it. He'd kidnapped Ayla's grandfather, her parents, *me*, and even Madison... all to increase his own leverage.

But something about that didn't feel complete, to me. He wasn't too concerned with keeping Madison alive, or he would've treated her wounds sooner. Yet me... I could tell he *wanted* to kill me. He was still clenching his fists tight, and there was tension in his jaw every time he looked at me, despite his haughty smirks. He *needed* me for something, and not just bait, because I was still breathing. As his guard friend had so eloquently pointed out, bait didn't have to be alive.

Was it because I was LeyGuard? The Hub *might* be more cautious, might demand proof of life before they made any deals. If so, I could use that... if I treaded carefully.

I met his gaze. "Madison needs help." I gestured to her leg. "Fadehound toxin."

Sevryn chuckled. "And I'm supposed to... what? Dash out of here with both of you in a rush of concern to save her? *This* is your threat?"

"No. I'm asking you to help her."

Sevryn tilted his head. "And if I *do*?"

I steeled myself and shrugged again. "You tell me. There must be something you want from me."

Sevryn laughed, but his eyes sparked with a mix of curiosity and eagerness—I was onto something.

Sevryn studied me. "Okay, LeyGuard, I'll bite." He chuckled, seeming to realize his own joke. "So what would be the terms of this *exchange*?"

I clenched Madison tighter. "That depends on what you want. I will not betray people I care about. I will not give you information on the Hub. I will not help you murder innocents, and I will not help you further your insane conquest of Teionyr."

Sevryn's jaw twitched. "That's quite a list of *will not*s, for someone begging me to save his friend's life."

"And yet you still haven't killed me." I examined his face, his stance, his still-clenched fists. He was guarding his reaction, calculating. Which meant none of what I'd just refused to give him was actually what he was after. *So then what?*

Sevryn watched me cautiously. "No... I suppose I have not."

"Madison is dying, Sevryn," I said, and watched his eyebrow twitch in annoyance at the casual way I addressed him. "We don't have time for this. What is it you *want* from me?" I slipped my hand toward my pocket. If things were about to go south, I still had the coin. I'd have to bust the ward, flash my fire, and hope I took Sevryn by surprise enough to rush out of here with Madison before he engaged his mind-sway.

To my surprise, Sevryn unclenched his fists and sighed. "I need your help to save the dying king."

I gaped at him. "What?"

"The king... is dying." Sevryn rolled his eyes. "How much clearer do I need to be?"

I raised an eyebrow. "You mean *Beirthyr*? The one who murdered his own brother, then cursed and framed his nephew to steal the throne? Why would I help you save *him*?"

Sevryn crossed his arms. "Because Teionyrian magic demands a seated royal on the throne, of the Teionyrian royal line. With the prince nowhere to be found, if the last of the royal line *dies*, the magical ward around the entire kingdom will be thrown into flux... and with it, the magic that sustains the remaining royals. Prince Kaizyn—*wherever* he's run off to—would be weakened, vulnerable. If something were to attack him... he could die." He let his words sink in, as well as the unspoken ones he wouldn't admit to: he knew *exactly* why Kaizyn wasn't here, and that he was bonded to Ayla. If Kaizyn died, she would, too.

He watched me. "I see you're piecing together some things," he said with a smirk. "Perhaps now you understand my position?"

With Beirthyr allied with the Selkbloods, invasion of Teionyr should have been easy. The fact that Sevryn hadn't just killed Beirthyr and poured armies of darklings in over the walls didn't make sense.

I shook my head. "I still don't get it. Why do you want to save him? Don't you *want* to take over Teionyr? Destroying the last of the royal magic would remove all protections keeping the Dark Fae armies out. You'd get exactly what you want."

His eyes narrowed. "You know very little about what I truly *want*."

I stepped back a moment, evaluating this turn in the conversation. He really did seem to want Beirthyr to live... for *some* reason. And though I didn't trust Sevryn in the least, what he said about the Teionyrian royal magic tracked with what I'd learned at the Hub. The Teionyrian magic system really *was* tied to having a seated royal on the throne, and the royals' power sustained the wards that protected the entire city. Without a seated ruler of the royal bloodline to sustain that barrier, Teionyr *would* fall to the Dark Fae armies already knocking at its doors. And as Teionyr's magic weakened, so would any royals who had come of age and completed their sear-bind ceremonies to attach to it... including Kaizyn. With Kaizyn's life tied to Ayla's, that was too much to risk—for Teionyr and for my heart.

I sucked a breath. "What would you need from me? I don't understand how I could even help."

Sevryn's eyes bored into mine for a moment, then he sighed and ran a hand through his dark hair. "When King Beirthyr ascended to the throne, he was required to complete the sear-bind ceremony to cement his connection to the heir-magic. He summoned quite a powerful fire-serpent from the Wilds. The Teionyrian people were greatly relieved to see that the throne had passed to such a powerful king; they held a marvelous ceremony in his honor."

I scoffed. "You mean, *you* threw a ceremony to convince the people that Beirthyr was their new, great protector... so that they wouldn't suspect that he's actually working with the very enemies trying to invade them."

Sevryn cut a glare at me. "With the former king dead and the heir-prince having fled under guilt of his murder, Beirthyr is Teionyr's *rightful* king."

I glared back, but chose not to comment. We both knew *that* was a farce.

"But now," Sevryn continued, "King Beirthyr's sear-bind has... turned on him."

"Does that *happen*?" The words shot out of me; I'd never heard of that occurring, even in all the hundreds of years of Upper Faeside history I'd had to wade through in my junior studies at the Hub. Teionyr had been subject to murders and coups before—what kingdom hadn't?—though never with the Dark Fae breathing down their necks as they were now. But still, even with previous coups, the magic *itself* had never turned against a royal who took the throne.

Sevryn shook his head. "Never before, according to Beirthyr himself. We've had to be *discreet,* of course, to avoid inciting a panic. The palace was emptied of all but Beirthyr's most trusted guards and council. We've separated the fire-serpent from him and contained it, but its very magic seems to be feeding on him, literally searing him alive from the inside out. Even Beirthyr's best mages have not been able to stop it."

I gaped at him. "And you think I can?"

"You are a LeyGuard from the House of Valos, are you not? You can command fire, and are trained in the runes and LeyGuard techniques to do so. Controlling fire-Fae magic is *literally* what your kind were created for."

He wasn't wrong, there... at least, not entirely. "I am a Wielder, not a Runist, Sevryn. I can use runes, yes, but I cannot draw them. It's not my branch of skill."

Sevryn nodded. "I am aware. I already have a Runist. A Wielder is what I need."

"You... already *have* a Runist?" I stared at him. Runing was a specialized skill, one that only about a third of LeyGuards in each House could master, and even then it had to be learned and perfected. Had he kidnapped another LeyGuard?

Sevryn waved a hand. "He's been here for ages; it seems the Hub has already forgotten to miss him."

*That* was strange... but only pulled me in deeper with curiosity. "So you will heal Madison, if I help you. And if I try, but cannot save Beirthyr? What happens then?"

His eyes narrowed. "It would be in both your and Madison's best interest for you not to fail."

I hadn't expected anything different. I swallowed. "And if I succeed?"

"Teionyr's magic will be stabilized, and you will return to my dungeons to await whatever arrangements your precious Hub or Ayla or the prince himself decides to bargain for you."

I eyed him. "Returned to the dungeons *alive*?"

Sevryn sighed. "Yes."

Despite what Sevryn implied about the Runist, the Hub didn't knowingly leave their own behind. The Hub would eventually make contact to bargain for my release. But I could only hope Ayla would stay far, far away from whatever shadiness was going down here in Teionyr, and let the Hub handle it. "And Madison?"

Sevryn shrugged. "Once I heal her, she's in your care. Keep her under control, and she may stay with you. If she causes trouble, I can make no guarantees."

My heart pounded as I studied his face. I didn't trust this Fae in the slightest, yet *something* bigger was happening here, and going deeper in was my best bet—both for saving Madison and figuring out why an invading force like the Selkbloods would be so bound and determined to keep the seated royal alive. And if what Sevryn said was true, if Beirthyr really was dying, helping him might also be the only way for me to save Kaizyn... and Ayla.

If I could get close to Beirthyr, maybe I could also learn more about the curse on Kaizyn, and the bond between him and Ayla. Perhaps I could even figure out how to unseat Beirthyr without harming Kaizyn or Teionyr, and return Kaizyn to his rightful throne. With an honorable royal on the throne, Teionyr stood a strong chance of repelling the Dark Fae armies indefinitely. If its royals were back at full strength, Teionyr could be a turning point for the entire war. Peace in the Fae lands... no more LeyGuards having to devote years to fighting Faeside, away from their families... no more fear of uprisings and breaches, for the LeyGuard *and* for Fae.

It could change everything. A chance for Ayla to live a normal life, safe from everything her grandfather had tried to protect her from. And maybe, even, a chance for me to live it *with* her.

I met his eyes again. "I will only try to stop whatever the sear-bind is doing—to save Beirthyr's life, for the sake of Teionyr's magic and Kaizyn's safety. I will not help your armies invade Teionyr. Once I save the king, my debt for you saving Madison is paid. Once you return us *alive* to the dungeons, my truce with you is void."

A smirk tugged at Sevryn's mouth. "A truce. Is that what this is?"

"Well, you are agreeing not to try to kill me, in exchange for my help, and I suppose I'm agreeing to the same. For now."

Sevryn nodded. "Very well." He slipped a vial of silvery liquid from his pocket and nodded toward Madison. "May I?"

I eyed the vial warily. He'd already had it with him. Had he been planning this exchange all along? Even if he had, it was too late now. Madison couldn't afford the time for me to renegotiate.

I laid Madison gently on the stone floor, though I stayed right at her side, just in case.

"I'm not going to kill her," Sevryn muttered. "For Void's sake, give me some space to work."

I scooted back a bit, still ready to move in if needed.

Sevryn uncorked the vial and dumped its contents onto Madison's wound.

Madison twitched and groaned. I lurched toward her.

"Patience!" Sevryn shot out his hand, blocking me.

I glared at his hand on my chest, and he quickly dropped it.

"The faespell takes a moment to work," he said. "It's uncomfortable, but it won't harm her."

I grudgingly settled back on my heels. Madison twitched again, and the purple streaks spreading out from the wound receded—the toxin was leaving her veins. I watched as the wound visible through the hole in her jeans knitted itself back together and the skin over it faded from angry red to glossy pink. She would definitely have a scar.

Madison stirred, then her eyes blinked open. She gasped as she saw Sevryn, but he moved back, giving me room to jump in.

"I'm here." I placed a hand on her shoulder. "You're okay."

Madison found me, and the panic in her eyes eased slightly. "Jordan?"

"I'm here." I squeezed her hand. "You're gonna be okay."

Her eyes drifted shut again, and I spun to look at Sevryn.

"It's normal." He shrugged. "The healing fuels itself using the body's own energy. She will need to rest, to regain her strength. I'll lead you both to another chamber, one where Madison can rest comfortably."

"And my magic? I'll need it to work, if I'm going to help you. You'll have to disable the ward." I had no intentions of escaping *immediately*—I was a man of my word—but if I could gain Sevryn's trust over the next however-long it took for me to complete my end of our deal, there might be a small window for escape once the truce was over, if I could convince him to keep me unwarded.

"You will be fitted with a ward-cuff before you leave the bounds of the prison, which will keep your magic dampened in your new chambers. When you are ready to use it, the cuff will be disabled for you to access your magic—with supervision."

I wasn't surprised, though that would make escaping a bit more of a challenge.

Sevryn narrowed his eyes at me. "This deal of ours requires a significant amount of restraint and trust on my part; I hope you realize that. But I will keep my side of our *truce*, and I intend you to do the same."

I held his gaze and nodded. "I will as long as you do." But when the truce was over, all bets were off. By then, I hoped to have learned enough to have a fresh new plan for busting out of here... and hopefully taking down Sevryn and Beirthyr's regime in the process.

Sevryn gave me a cold grin. "I look forward to when the truce is lifted."

I glared back at him. "So do I."

C H A P T E R 6

# What's Right in Front of You

***Striker***

Rory Kane was pale in all the wrong places and bruised in all the *other* places. He looked like an elephant had stepped on him, kicked him a few times, then stabbed him in the back for good measure. Knowing the things that lived in this part of the Veil, that might not have been too far off from reality.

I knelt down beside him, ignoring the way his blood clung to my boots. "What happened to him? That thing outside?"

Callan ran a weary hand through his hair. "No. That caught up to us when I tried to move him." He knelt down beside me, leveling a concerned stare at Rory's face. "I don't know what did this. He was already hurt when I found him."

I scanned Rory but couldn't see any obvious wounds on the front of his body, nothing to account for the puddle he was lying in. "Where's the blood coming from? Did you apply pressure?"

Callan sighed and stood. "Upper back. Near his shoulder blade. And I tried. The bleeding slowed, and I had it bandaged, but it reopened when that thing chased us, I think. We had to move fast. I—I wasn't as gentle as I should have been." He sounded shaken.

I glanced up at Callan. Fae weren't usually this easily unsettled. A guard like Callan would be no stranger to injuries or blood... or to hideous creatures jumping out at him from the Void.

He seemed to notice my evaluating glance. His jaw clenched, and his next words came out as a tight whisper: "I can't let him die."

Oh. *Right*. He and Rory's sister... I huffed a short laugh as things clicked into place. "Yeah. I imagine that would put a damper on your relationship, a bit."

I forgot, sometimes, that Callan was still a kid. A *Fae* kid—trained as a guard from birth, and as lethal in his teens as any full-grown human assassin—but still a kid, hoping not to have to tell his new girlfriend he let her brother die in front of him.

I put my hands on Rory's shoulder and waist, then looked up at Callan. "Help me turn him on his side."

Callan let out a shaky huff and dropped back into a kneel beside me, resting his hands on Rory's hip and legs. "Voids, that's a lot of blood."

I grunted my assent as we tipped Rory gently onto his side so I could look for the wound. *There*. Near the shoulder blade, as Callan had said. His shirt was torn, and the bandage beneath it was soaked through, blood trailing down Rory's shirt and back. I peeled off the bandage. It immediately started bleeding more profusely. I winced. Rory's shoulder was practically flayed open.

"It's bad," I said, "but not in a place that's likely to be lethal... that is, unless it gets infected, or there's internal damage deeper in that I can't see, or we just stand around here and let him bleed to death." I reached for my pack, then remembered I'd tossed both bags to the girl. Lands alive—I was getting rusty in my old age. "Got any sutures? More bandages? Any supplies? A faespell would be *really* nice about now."

Callan shook his head. "I already used my emergency kit on him. It's all I had. I didn't have time to grab supplies before—" He paused. "The hound took Madison, and I thought maybe I could catch up to them. There wasn't much time to think."

I nodded. "We'll make do." I slipped my hunting knife from its holster and used it to tear some strips from the front of Rory's shirt, the part that wasn't soaked with blood, then started knotting them together into one long strip.

As I tied, I said, "There are others in here, too. Reina—Ayla. Maybe even that dog. Have you seen them?"

"Ayla should be fine," Callan said. "She had the stone, and as soon as she breached Kaizyn would've felt her. He wouldn't have let her get far without help. I wouldn't have sent her in without me if I hadn't known that." He glanced at me in concern. "But the others weren't with her? She's alone?"

I grunted. "Wasn't meant to be. I got a little delayed. But Ayla said Reina got pulled through without her. The dog, too. You haven't seen them?"

Callan shook his head. "No." He looked worried.

I sighed. "Reina's tough. Hopefully she found her way to a LeyGate and already got herself out of here. Even better if she also took the dog." I finished tying the strips and nodded toward Rory. "You hold him, I'll bandage."

Callan held Rory steady as I pulled the skin around his wound together as best I could, then applied a new makeshift bandage by wrapping the strip across the wound, then under his armpit and over the top of his opposite shoulder, tight, to keep pressure on the wound. The bleeding slowed to a trickle, but the bandage would be soaked through again in no time. We'd have to be careful how we moved him, yet also move quickly, somehow. Rory couldn't afford much more time to bleed.

"Nearest outpost I know is way too far," I said grimly, then glanced up at Callan. "You know a closer place we can take him, some place with medics, or healers, or at least supplies?"

Callan's mouth pulled into a tight line, and he eyed me, like he was trying to decide something. His gaze bounced to Rory's bloody shoulder. He drew a quick breath and nodded. "Yeah. I know a place. He'll be safe there until we get more help."

"All right, then," I hoisted Rory into my arms and stood. He was heavy, but still just a teen—nothing I couldn't carry, at least for a while. I turned to Callan and found him watching us grimly. "Callan?" My call seemed to break his trance.

He met my eyes. "Do you think Madison is still alive, wherever they took her?"

I could see the questions tormenting him, the ones all soldiers ask: Could I have been faster? Could I have been more careful? Could I have prevented this? *Did I make the right choices?*

I'd never believed in lying just to spare a kid's feelings, and I didn't plan to start now. "No way of knowing for sure," I said, then jutted my chin toward Rory. "Best you can do is leave regret in the past, leave what you don't know yet to the future, and do as much good as you can with what's right in front of you."

Callan's glance cut to Rory, and by the time he looked back at me, something in his eyes had shifted. "Yes. Yes, of course." He turned toward the cave's mouth. "Come, hurry. If we're lucky, we can be there before the rest of the herd catches our scent."

I followed Callan out of the cave, tucking Rory's limp body against my chest as I ducked through the entrance. "Herd? I'm not sure I like the sound of that."

Callan turned to me. "You shouldn't. That beast you killed? They travel in herds. That one peeled off to chase us while the rest were distracted, but the others can't be far behind."

*Fantastic.* Then it occurred to me: "Distracted by *what*?"

Callan gave me a cold smile. "Something much worse. Let's just say Rory and I got the better end of that scenario." His smile faded. "But there were enough of these beasts, I'm sure some survived. They'll be looking for their dead companion."

I glanced toward the pile of ash that used to be the dino-beast. "They do that?"

Callan shrugged. "They have before." He slid his knife out, and as he moved into the darkness, a stalking, panther-like awareness returned to his stance—a Fae warrior's stance. It brought a grin to my face. Whatever mild panic Callan had been dealing with, he'd shoved it to the back—like a true warrior—to do what needed to be done.

He glanced back at me, and I gave him a nod. "We'll save Rory, kid, then we'll find out what happened to Madison and the others."

A glint like flame on steel flashed behind his eyes. "Yes. We will." He returned my nod and gestured for me to follow. "Let's go."

# Chapter 7

# Not Ever

*Ayla*

Kaizyn helped me hobble inside the cave, then settled me on a big, flat rock over to one side of the space, almost like a stone bench. "Comfortable?"

I was sitting on a hard rock, but it was better than standing on my hurt ankle, so I nodded.

Kaizyn gave me a gentle smile. "Good. One moment."

The cave was fairly deep but only one room, with a low mattress on one side topped with a rumpled pile of blankets, and a small table and shelves on the other side. The shelves' contents were visible only as shadowy, irregular shapes in the faint glow of the light Kaizyn had conjured near me. Some of them looked like jars, others like books.

There was a large barrel near the table, like the wooden kegs of ale I'd seen in pirate movies, and beside that was a small cooking-stove. The cave didn't seem vented anywhere, but the stove looked portable, so maybe Kaizyn cooked outside. Beside the stove stood another shelf, stocked with a couple of pots and some metal dishes, something that resembled a teakettle, and some jars of what looked like food and cooking supplies, with a wash-basin on top.

Kaizyn's cave reminded me a little of a Hobbit-hole, only made from rock instead of dug into earth and grass.

Through the edges of the curtain that covered the opening, I could glimpse the orange-pink glow of Vyrthil—in his muted form, now, not full-blaze—pacing outside the entrance to our cave. I felt safer inside with a fire-cat as a guard. Almost like I could relax, for the first time since I'd entered the Veil.

Kaizyn scooped some liquid from the barrel with a ladle, then poured it into a metal cup and brought it to me. "Not all water in the Veil is safe to drink, but this is. I gathered it myself, from a spring nearby."

I took the cup from him and sipped. The water tasted crisp, though it was lukewarm, the same temperature as the air of the Veil itself. I drank the water gratefully—I hadn't realized how dry my throat was.

Kaizyn reached for the cup. "More?"

I shook my head. "I'm fine, thank you."

He smiled politely and carried the cup over to the wash-basin near the stove.

This was awkward, playing house-guest to a Fae I barely knew. As Kaizyn hand-washed and dried the cup, I looked around the details of the space, again, and... I was impressed. Kaizyn seemed to have made a home of this place, despite the fact that he was *cursed* to be in the Veil. "How long have you been here?"

"A few weeks—since around the time you first saw me in the café. But once we realized I might be stuck here for some time, Callan did his best to smuggle me supplies, so I would have a comfortable place to stay." He set the cup on the shelf, then turned toward me and smiled. "He's a far better friend than I deserve."

I smiled back at him. "From what Callan said, he considers you more than worthy of his loyalty and help. He spoke of you as both his ruler and... something like a brother. Like family. He said you were a good man."

"As is he," Kaizyn said, and his smile faded. "I hope he is all right. You said he went to help someone?"

"Madison, yes. She was taken by some kind of Fae monster thing."

Realization, mixed with something like fear, crossed Kaizyn's face. "Madison. Oh."

From the way he said it, I could tell he knew what Madison meant to Callan—maybe even more than I'd realized.

Kaizyn clenched and unclenched a fist, like a nervous habit. "What did you say took her?"

"A Fadehound? At least, that's what I think Callan said he thought it was."

Kaizyn cursed under his breath, words I couldn't make out, then he exhaled slowly. "If anyone can save her, it will be Callan. He's a skilled warrior, deadly as a sharpened blade."

I blinked at him, trying to reconcile that with my images of Callan at school, and of him flirting with Madison. I could see it, if I tried, the ferocity beneath the surface. I'd seen enough of Callan's Fae side already that I could extrapolate the rest. But I never would've guessed he was a trained, deadly Fae warrior when I'd first met him at school. Callan was good at blending in.

I was glad he was on *our* side.

Kaizyn knelt by my feet. "We should address your injury," he said, looking up at me. "Do you mind?"

I realized after a second that he was asking if it was okay for him to remove my shoe to see my foot and ankle, so I nodded. "Sure, go ahead."

Kaizyn's hands were gentle as he slid off my shoe and sock—I could only hope my feet weren't smelly, though if they were, there wasn't much I could do about it now—and slid the edge of my jeans up slightly, so he could examine my ankle.

The ankle throbbed, and the swelling and bruising were apparent. I'd definitely injured it, though whether it was a sprain or something worse, I couldn't say.

Kaizyn tilted it gently, then prodded tenderly around the joints, careful not to cause me too much pain. His fingers moved expertly, like he knew what he was looking for.

I watched him with curiosity, which he must have felt, because he glanced up at me. "You have a question." It was a statement; he knew I wanted to ask something.

*That* was still unsettling; I wasn't sure I'd ever get used to him reading me like that. But I shrugged it off and asked my question, anyway. "Do you have medical training? You seem like you've done this before."

Kaizyn went back to prodding my ankle as he answered. "Royals in Teionyr are trained in many things. We often go to battle with our armies, so in times of war, it behooves our people for the royals to be versatile in our skills. Kings and princes should be assets to their armies, not liabilities." He looked up at me. "I was born in a time of war, so I am trained in many wartime skills. I am not *good* at all of them"—he laughed softly—"but I have been trained in them. Healing, however, was one I always did well. My teachers said I had a natural aptitude for reading the body, for knowing what it needs."

I tilted my head, slipping that new jigsaw-piece of information into the puzzle of Kaizyn slowly coming together in my mind.

"Your ankle is sprained." Kaizyn hurried to the other side of the cave and grabbed some items off the shelf, then knelt in front of me and spread the items out on the floor: a cloth wrap, similar to what I would've used at home to bind a swollen ankle, and a couple small vials of glistening liquid, one opalescent and the other a pale blue.

I gasped. "Are those—"

His gaze followed mine, then he smiled up at me. "No, nothing like the faespell that bound us." His smile slipped. "I'm afraid I have nothing that will actually *heal* you—all the strongest faespells are behind guard at the palace. Callan was able to find me some lesser faespells, though. One of these should help with swelling, and the other will reduce pain. You will still have to be careful as your injury heals."

He pressed around my ankle a bit more deeply, which was uncomfortable but not overly painful, then he looked up at me. "I'm going to apply the serums for swelling and pain now, if that's all right?"

I nodded. "Of course." At this point, I trusted he wasn't trying to poison me... if I died, so did he, right? Besides, I'd already activated the most awkward faespell possible on us when I accidentally bound us. Compared to that, the risks seemed low.

Kaizyn unstoppered the vials one at a time, dousing my ankle and foot in each one. The relief was immediate, and so was the external change. The swelling receded, and some of the blue and purple discoloration faded away, as well.

"Wow." I rotated my ankle slowly—it still ached, but the throbbing had stopped. I slid forward and carefully put some weight on the foot. I no longer got a sharp pain when I put pressure on it. "That's much better." I smiled at him. "Thank you."

Kaizyn returned my smile. "You're welcome." He cut off a length of cloth strip from the roll on the floor with his knife, wrapped my ankle with it, then tied it off and slid my jeans back down over it. "It would be good for you to leave your sock and shoe off for a bit," he said, "and to put your leg up and rest it, while you can. Elevating it with a pillow would be best. Perhaps you could use my—" Kaizyn glanced at his bed, and a faint blush tinged his cheeks. He hurried over, straightening the blankets. "I—my apologies. Father always said that a state of a man's chambers reflected the state of his life, but I suppose that naturally, I am not quite as tidy as—I mean—"

A soft laugh escaped me at this frenzied prince, capable of decapitating a feral lizard-beast to save me, yet worried about his bed-making skills. For a moment, I could almost picture Kaizyn as just a regular teenager who hated making his bed. Almost.

He turned at the sound of my laugh, and I smiled. "Kaizyn, it's fine." I actually found it somewhat comforting that a Fae prince could be self-conscious about forgetting to make his bed—it made him seem almost *normal.*

Another blush crept up his neck, and he shrugged, though he returned my smile. "I'm not used to guests in my... personal quarters."

I smiled wider at that. "Me neither, actually. I think the only people who have ever been in my bedroom are my parents and grandpa... and maybe Reina, a few times, when we were little." Concern for Reina swept in at me. The last I'd seen her, she'd been sucked into the Veil right in front of me.

I forced a breath. Kaizyn would help me find her—find *all* of them—but first, I needed to rest my ankle so I could walk properly and I wouldn't get both Kaizyn and myself killed.

I kept rambling, trying to drown out the worries looming in the back of my mind. "Really, it's fine. I'm not the tidiest, either. I usually have a pile of books on my nightstand, maybe some clothes over my desk chair, and I don't always make my bed." I ended the statement with an awkward laugh... because, of course, I was *me.*

A line formed between Kaizyn's eyebrows as he stared at me in confusion, and I realized he must be sensing my wild fluctuation of emotions without understanding the cause.

He opened his mouth like he wanted to ask me about them, then sighed. "This is not how I envisioned our first meeting, and I do not wish you to judge me based on... this." He swept his hand, indicating he meant the cave. "Father always chided me for my untidiness. At the palace, of course, we have helpers—not servants; we do not believe in that. We pay our palace workers well. But father always said that when I married, I would need a helper to tidy our space, so that my future queen would not have to live in my mes—"

The realization that *I* was now that future queen, as far as his kingdom laws were concerned, hit me squarely in the chest.

Kaizyn stopped mid-sentence, alarm on his face.

He must've felt my panic, and this time, he knew exactly what had caused it.

"I'm sorry," he said in a rush. "I didn't mean—" He took a tentative step toward me. "Ayla, you know I would never *force* you, right? No matter what the laws say, I will not force you to become my wife." He was near me now, hovering over me as I sat on the stone bench.

From what I understood, a deep faespell-bond like this one—where he felt my every emotion—meant I was the *only* woman Kaizyn could marry. If he was bonded to me but I didn't marry him, he would be forced to remain alone. It was hard to believe he would be okay with that.

I forced myself to meet his gaze. "Not even if the bond can't be broken?"

Those deep blue eyes stared into mine in a way that cracked deep into my chest. "Not even then. Not ever."

# Chapter 8

# Safe, Body and Soul

*Ayla*

I didn't feel attached to Kaizyn the way Callan had said Kaizyn felt about me. I barely *knew* him. But in that moment, I could *feel* him—not specific emotions, like he could feel from me... but his sincerity, a solidity, like the bond was showing me the truth of his heart. And I knew, right then, that I could trust him.

I let out a long breath. "Okay."

"You believe me," Kaizyn said, still holding my gaze. "I can feel it."

I nodded. "Yes."

A smile lit his face, so joyful it sent a little thrill through my chest. Then he gently grabbed my hand. His eyes were intense as he stared down at me. "I will never betray that belief, Ayla Rogers. I know the bond is strange for you—I am still learning it, myself. But I will never speak falsely to you, and I will never begrudge you your own thoughts and feelings, no matter how they might... pain me." He gave my hand a gentle squeeze, then slid his hand away and stepped back, giving me space, though his eyes still held mine with a deep intensity. "With me, you are safe, body and soul. Even if it breaks my own heart."

My breath caught at those last words—because he knew about Jordan. How could he not? He had felt it through our bond. Kaizyn knew I couldn't return his feelings, that I couldn't ever marry him. Yet I could feel the purity of his heart as he spoke—he genuinely meant every word. I was safe with him. In every way.

I stared up at him, at a loss for words. "Thank you." What else could I say?

Kaizyn stepped away. "You should rest and elevate your leg. My bed is a mess, as we established"—he let out a little laugh—"but you are welcome to use it. I've not slept much lately. Besides a few minutes of tossing fitfully on them, my bed things are mostly clean. Or I could bring you some pillows and a blanket over here instead if you prefer."

The thought of lying in his bed felt a little *too* familiar, but some padding did sound good to my aching backside and tired muscles. "Pillows and a blanket would be fine."

Kaizyn helped me stretch my legs out sideways on the bench. He propped my back up with one pillow and placed another pillow under my injured foot. Then he handed me his blanket. "In case you get cold, or need extra padding for your leg."

I took the blanket, and his scent enveloped me from it, a warm, woodsy sort of smell from his fire magic, reminiscent of summer cookouts on my dad's wood-burning grill. The thought sent a wave of homesickness through me. "It smells like you," I said without really thinking.

Kaizyn studied me, his expression unreadable, then took a step backward. "You'll be safe here—Vyrthil and I will keep watch. I know we need to find your friends, and I am eager to learn more about what happened before you came here. But for now, please, rest. Quiet moments are few in the Veil. I can feel that you're tired, and faespells pull from the body's strength to activate their magic. You'll soon be feeling that drain. You should rest."

Everything in me wanted to jump up and run after my friends, but—he was right. Now that I was sitting still, I felt bone-weary. I doubted I could march very far through the Veil at the moment, even if I were being chased again. I sighed. "Okay. Thank you."

"You're welcome." Kaizyn smiled, and though it didn't quite reach his eyes, I could still feel it was sincere. He turned away, then turned back. His eyes met mine as he added quietly, like an afterthought: "I know we cannot be more, but I hope we will be friends."

Staring back into those deep blue eyes, I genuinely wanted that, too. I wanted to know him, to be friends with him, even if it was complicated. I could see why Callan was so loyal to him—and why it was so important for Kaizyn to be returned to the throne. I could see he was *good*. "I would like that, too," I said. "I could always use another quality friend."

I was amassing more of them, lately, than I'd ever thought possible—*if* the others were still okay. If we could get them back.

Kaizyn must've felt the sudden wave of sadness and concern that swept over me. His eyes softened. "You miss them."

Hot tears pressed behind my eyes as I nodded back. "Yes."

Kaizyn reached out and gently squeezed my hand. "I will help you find them, Ayla. You have my word."

A small thread of peace settled into my soul, because I could tell he meant that, too.

"But first," Kaizyn said, "you should rest. Sleep, if you'd like. I promise to wake you in a short while, or sooner, if something happens. But you're too tired to go back out there, right now, and we will *both* need strength for later."

A tremor of concern moved through me at the way he said that. "You said my emotions are so strong they sometimes feel like you're feeling them yourself... Does my exhaustion make you tired, too?"

I couldn't read his expression, but true to his word, he didn't lie to me. "Sometimes. But my struggles are my own, Ayla. Don't worry about me. Just rest." He turned away, busy clearing away the empty vials and putting away the roll of cloth.

My thoughts swirled like a whirlwind, but I forced myself to relax back onto the pillow. Despite all my anxieties, Kaizyn was right... I'd be no good to anyone with a hurt ankle *and* too tired to walk straight, especially if my exhaustion fed over into him.

Kaizyn's life depended on mine, his emotions depended on mine... What a strange conundrum I found myself in, *me*, who struggled to even identify my own needs and constantly pushed my exhaustion or feelings aside. Now, what I felt could literally make or break another person. It was... way, way too much pressure.

I saw Kaizyn flinch, a tightening in his back and shoulders, and I realized he'd felt my surge of overwhelm, too. But he said nothing. Again, he bore my emotional train wreck without blaming me or saying a word.

*Great.* Being bound to Kaizyn was like having a screaming, neon sign thrust in my face about how much I needed to learn to deal with my feelings, instead of shoving everything down. I sighed. My feelings were too big of a mess to sort through right now, but I should at least try to rest, so I wouldn't get us both killed. Plus, unless he could also read my dreams, my sleep would probably be a blessed silence for Kaizyn since there would be no crazy emotions screaming at him.

As though he read my mind—which I was sure he partly did—Kaizyn said softly, "I'm glad you're here, Ayla. It is nice... to have a friend here."

He didn't look at me as he spoke, but I could feel he meant it, and it hit me like a wave of peace. I could trust him—with *all* my crazy, because heaven knew I couldn't hide any of it from him. But he accepted it without judgment. He accepted *me*. And I knew I would accept him, too—no matter how awkward or messy it got, I would be honest with him. I would trust him.

I wouldn't *marry* him—the thought of *that* still sent a shock of panic through me—but I would make sure I was every bit as trustworthy a friend to him as he was to me. I wouldn't abandon him in this Void. I would find the cure to release him from his curse, and to put him back on his throne, and to break this bond so he could be *free*, if those were the last things I did.

And because I knew Jordan so well, too, I knew he would be completely on board; he would help me—once we found him. And we *would* find him, because I refused to accept any future without Jordan in it. I might be bound to Kaizyn, but I knew for sure now, if I hadn't before... I was in love with Jordan Peters. Not even a magical Fae bond could compete with how I felt about him.

Kaizyn spun toward me, and regret seared through me as I realized he'd probably felt all of *that*, too—but his expression wasn't pain or alarm. It was warrior-steel.

He held up a hand, gesturing for me to be still. "There's something outside," he whispered, then he slid his sword from its sheath and crept silently toward the cave mouth. With a wave of his fingers, he doused the orb of light, and darkness swallowed us.

Vyrthil's orange glow flickered at one edge of the curtained opening, then vanished. I pushed up to sit, readying myself to run or hide if needed, and tried to steady my breathing.

I could hear Kaizyn's breaths wisping, faint and even, as tense silence washed over us. I timed my breaths to his, as a way of holding back the fear. One breath, *in, out*. Another breath, *in, out*. Another—

"Stay here," Kaizyn whispered, then the curtain rustled as he slipped outside.

I pulled further into myself, drawing shallow breaths, listening, trying not to panic.

A feral shriek sliced the silence outside, then a wall of flame surged into the mouth of the cave, burning the curtain to ash. A wave of heat slammed toward me.

I curled against the stone wall and screamed.

The air crackled, then shattered. Tiny crystals rained down around me. One hit the bench, and I stared at it, confused. *Ice?* I glanced up—

And there, beyond the glinting bits of ice that now littered the cave floor, stood Kaizyn, Striker, and Callan in the cave door—all gaping at me.

Striker stepped inside the cave, chewing the match in the corner of his mouth. He looked down at the floor, then looked back up at me. "Kid—" His eyes narrowed. "Did you just do *magic*?"

I stared at Striker. I was glad to see him, but—"Magic? *Me?* No!" That was crazy, right?

Striker stepped toward me. "Ayla, we just sent a wall of flame toward this cave to kill a lizard-beast that almost got in here, and when it flared unexpectedly—explosive little buggers—we all thought you were about to be roasted. Now, I'm from Valos, like Jordan. I have fire magic." He pointed to his own chest. "See them?" He gestured to Kaizyn and Callan. "Teionyrian. Fire-Fae. Not a one of us in this cave—except apparently you—can make ice." He grinned at me. "I am relieved to see you safe, though."

"What?" I shook my head. "No, I don't have magic. It wasn't me." *Could it have been?*

Callan stepped toward me, slowly, like he didn't want to startle me. "You are LeyGuard by birth, Ayla. It is *possible.*"

Possible? Sure. My best friends were LeyGuards, my *Grandpa* was some kind of LeyGuard hero, Fae monsters had kidnapped my family and friends, I could hear voices in my mind, and now I was magically bound to a Fae prince—I'd learned that *anything* was possible these last two weeks. But... me with *magic*? Somehow that strained the edges of believability, even for me.

Callan glanced back at Striker.

Striker hurled a fireball at me without warning.

"No!" Kaizyn dove for me, to intercept it, just as I screamed—

The fireball shattered, exploding into an icy mist.

Kaizyn landed in front of me, then spun and charged at Striker. "How *dare* you! That could've—"

"Could've." Striker stopped Kaizyn with an outstretched hand, then grinned at me. "But didn't."

Kaizyn sucked a deep breath, still seething, then turned slowly toward me, taking in my uninjured face, and my hair—which was dusted in quickly melting powder, almost like a thin snow.

The ice-residue of the fireball I'd destroyed.

His anger twisted into something like disbelief or confusion.

Striker smiled at him. "The kid's got magic. See?"

Behind him, Callan's eyes widened.

Kaizyn stepped toward me. "Ayla?"

I raised a hand in front of my face. Tendrils of white vapor smoked up from my fingernails, like the mist when you open a freezer in a warm room.

A tremor of excitement built in my chest as I looked up at Kaizyn. "I think—I think maybe I *do*."

## CHAPTER 9

# TRUST YOUR GUT

**Jordan**

Sevryn waited for me to pick Madison back up—she was *my* responsibility now—then led me down the short corridor to another sealed door.

He tapped on the door, and a guard in royal regalia inched it open, blocking the opening. "Yes, Lord Sevryn?"

"Fetch me two ward-cuffs." Sevryn's speech was abrupt and demanding, but apparently the guard was used to it, because he didn't bat an eye.

"Yes, my lord." He hurried off.

Sevryn shut the door, and we waited a few moments in awkward silence, the tension of our newly formed truce hanging thick in the air between us, until the guard returned and edged the door open, shoving two metal cuffs through.

Sevryn took the cuffs, and the door slammed shut again, the guard hidden on the other side.

Sevryn turned to me. "Your wrist."

I ignored his snippy tone and stuck out one arm. Sevryn fitted the cuff around my wrist, then snapped it shut. It sealed smooth, like a metal bracelet, but with no hinge in sight. "How does it come off?"

Sevryn raised an eyebrow. "By my command. Now her." He jutted his chin toward Madison.

I blinked. "The other cuff is for *her*? She doesn't even have magic!"

Sevryn narrowed his eyes. "I don't take chances." He lifted one of Madison's limp arms and snapped the cuff in place. "There. Now follow me." He yanked open the door and strode into the hallway.

I shifted Madison's weight and followed.

The guard from moments earlier was nowhere in sight. A long, empty corridor stretched out before us, mostly stone walls, with windows high up which let in streams of sunlight. Thin, green vines twisted around the edges of one of the window frames, visible through the barred glass. There were no decorations in the hallway, though that wasn't surprising for prison corridors. I assumed we were in what amounted to the palace's dungeon, though it clearly wasn't all below ground.

There was a bend in the corridor ahead, but before we reached it, Sevryn stopped at a door in the wall—the first door I'd seen in this hallway. He shoved the door open. "Your chambers will be in here." The room inside was dark, lit only by the faint glow of a lantern on the wall to the right of the door. The rest of the room was shadowed.

I stepped inside, Madison still in tow, and turned back toward the hall.

Sevryn filled the doorway. "Enjoy your stay. Get to know your new roommate. I'll summon you when it's time to see the king." He slammed the door shut in my face.

*Our roommate?* I turned back to the room, straining to hear any sound of movement as my eyes adjusted to the darkness.

When my eyes did adjust, I could make out the faint shape of a bed a few steps ahead of me. It seemed empty and safe enough, so I laid Madison down on it carefully, then spun back to grab the lantern. Light source in hand, I hurried back to Madison's side, then turned slowly, seeking our so-called *roommate*. I couldn't make out anything in the shadows, and I didn't dare leave Madison's side long enough to explore the room, not without knowing who else was in there. "Hello?"

A prolonged grunt came from the far corner. "Leave me alone, Fae scum."

The voice was gruff but slightly warbled, like an old man. He didn't *sound* all that dangerous, but I knew better than to let down my guard. I held the light up and took one step toward the voice, still within reach of Madison. "I'm not *Fae scum*. I'm a LeyGuard. Who are you?"

I heard a scuffle, and when the voice spoke again, it sounded nearer. "LeyGuard, are you? Hmph. Which House?"

I moved the light, searching, but still couldn't see anyone. "Valos."

The man let out a rough laugh. "Where's your flame then, boy?"

I held up my ward-cuff. "Doused... for the moment."

The man grunted again—and then he was right in my face, putrid breath puffing against my nostrils. "You don't say."

I scurried backward in surprise, the back of my legs bumping the bed as the lantern swung overhead.

The man howled in laughter. "What are they teaching you LeyGuards these days? I nearly made it up your nostrils before you spotted me!"

The room suddenly flooded with light, and I threw up one hand to protect my stinging eyes.

My eyes recovered, and I lowered my hand to find an old, hunched man in a baggy tunic and torn pants staring at me. Above us, an electric light—or something similar, perhaps powered by magic—bathed the room in a corn-yellow glow. The room was small, with stone walls and no windows, containing the narrow bed I'd placed Madison on and one other bed, with an armoire between and a lavatory of sorts in the far corner. The man's laughter simmered into a low chuckle as he stared at me, grinning.

My anger flared. "Why didn't you *tell* me there was a light switch?"

The man shrugged. "Gotta entertain myself somehow. Don't get many guests in here, you know."

Some of my anger faded. The man seemed harmless enough—though maybe a bit off his rocker. I sank onto the edge of the bed. "We aren't guests. We're roommates. I'm guessing we'll be here for a while."

The man smiled, sadly. "Well, I'm sorry for that, then. What did you do to get thrown in here with a madman like me?"

The man's easy-going demeanor set off red flags. I didn't know him; I couldn't trust him. Better if I gave him as little information as possible. "I'd rather not say."

The man eyed me. "Wise enough. Never know whom you can trust." He inched around and sat on the bed opposite me. Our knees nearly touched in the cramped space, but I resisted the urge to pull away. The man's gaze slid past me, to Madison, but to my relief, there was no threat in his stare, only concern. "What happened to your friend?" he asked.

I chewed the inside of my lip, debating how much to tell him, but I couldn't see any harm in the truth. "She was bitten by a Fadehound. She's been treated, but Sevryn said it may take her some time to wake."

The man's eyes slid from Madison's face to mine. "She LeyGuard, too?"

My jaw clenched, but for some reason, I answered him. "No. Just an innocent human, caught up in my mess."

The man sighed. "That's too bad." He seemed sincere. "Perhaps she'll make it out of this all right." His watery, grey eyes met mine. "Valos House, is it? Mind if I ask what kind of deal you made? They don't bring just any prisoner to this room, even if they *are* LeyGuard."

I eyed him. "I'd rather not say... at least, not until I understand why *you* are here. I don't even know who you are."

The old man stared at my face for a solid two minutes, until I became rather uncomfortable, then he sighed. "I'm Etcher."

I laughed. "*Etcher*? As in, the legendary Valos Runist from the early Upper Faeside war? The one who literally wrote the LeyGuard *textbook* on fire runes? That's not possible. He's—"

"Dead?" Now it was the old man's turn to laugh. "Yeah... perhaps not as much as expected, though being trapped in this room for decades is its own kind of death."

I gaped at him. "No. Not possible." For all I knew, he could *believe* he was Etcher, but if so... "You'd be over a hundred years old!"

"A hundred and fifty, give or take a few," the old man said with a shrug. He raised one sleeve, revealing a wrinkled arm... with a rune tattooed on it.

I studied the rune. "I've never seen one like that before."

The man dropped his sleeve. "That's because it's an original. Long-life rune. First and only of its kind. Although, once I got to this place, I kind of regretted having it. Got captured in the last war. Figured they'd fake my death—a Runist like me is too valuable an asset for the Dark Fae for them to risk the LeyGuard trying to steal me back." He rubbed his arm and grumbled. "Really should've crafted it for long *youth*, though. Instead, I just got old and stayed that way."

"And you... help the Dark Fae here?" I stared at him. "Why?"

Something dark moved in behind his eyes. "I have my reasons, boy. Same as you have yours. But you can trust me. I'll watch out for you, in here. The LeyGuard protects its own."

I glanced at Madison on the bed, then swallowed. "Okay. Sure. But how do I know I really can trust you?"

The old man cocked his head at me. "You trust your gut, as always. Or did you get yourself captured before the LeyGuard taught you how?"

There was derision in his question, but oddly enough, it centered me. I *did* trust my gut—it was what told me Ayla's family could be rescued, what led me to take the risk that did, in fact, save them... even if it got me captured. I'd gone in, knowing that risk, but also trusting my instinct that the rescue was possible. I might still be in training, but my instincts had always been strong—stronger even than the Hub council's, sometimes. Or maybe they just weren't willing to do what was necessary, even if they knew what it was.

I eyed the old man. He was irritating and possibly crazy, but who wouldn't have been, after being trapped here for decades? More importantly, I *did* have a gut instinct about him... and it said I could trust him. I supposed, in my current circumstances, that was the best assurance I would get for now.

Not that I wouldn't still be wary.

"Well?" he said.

"Well, *what*?"

"Do you believe me?"

I sighed. "Despite myself... yeah, I kind of do." I hesitated a moment, then held out my hand. "I'm Jordan."

He grinned and shook my hand. "Well then, I'm glad to meet you, Jordan of Valos."

A smile crept to my lips. "Same to you, Etcher."

The door banged open, and Etcher and I both spun toward it.

A guard I didn't recognize stood in the doorway. "Lord Sevryn is ready for you—both of you." He glanced between Etcher and me.

I tensed. "I'm not leaving Madison."

The guard shrugged. "Suit yourself, but you carry her." He turned back to the hallway. "Follow me and try to keep up."

I hoisted Madison back over my shoulder and hurried after the guard, Etcher trailing behind us with quick, shuffling steps.

The guard didn't care that Etcher was old, or that I was carrying another person. He hurried on ahead, expecting us to follow. He turned a corner, then turned again at the end of the corridor. We barely made it to that corner in time to see him turn yet again.

I shifted Madison and tried to hurry, but I also didn't want to leave Etcher behind.

"Don't worry," Etcher said from a few steps behind me, his voice strained and out of breath. "I know where they're taking us. It's just around the corner ahead. And they'll wait—they need us, after all. Even so, no need upsetting them by dallying. It only complicates things."

I wasn't sure I wanted to know what he meant by that, so I conserved my breath.

He was right, though. When we turned the next corner, the guard was waiting there beside an open door with an annoyed look on his face.

"Took you long enough. In here." The guard gestured to the doorway.

I waited for Etcher to catch up, then we stepped inside.

The room was ornate, with a massive, curtained bed in the center of the room—gold velvet curtains drawn around it, obscuring any occupant—with elaborate crystal-and-gold chandeliers overhead and an over-whelming amount of red and gold patterned wallpaper on every wall.

The door slammed behind us with a sense of finality.

Sevryn rose from where he lounged in a plush, red velvet chair to our left, beside an ornate, gold-edged cherry-wood vanity with an elaborate gold-framed mirror.

I had the passing thought that perhaps he'd just been sitting there, staring at himself—I wouldn't put it past him. I stifled the smile that tried to creep up, and met Sevryn's stare.

"You are here to do a job," he said brusquely, shifting his gaze between Etcher and me. "You will not converse unnecessarily, you will not waste time, and you will not leave this room until I'm satisfied with your work. If you speak a word of what happens within this room to *anyone* else in this palace, even the guards, I will kill you on the spot. Do you both understand?"

Etcher sighed. "Yes, yes, the usual. Can we get on with it? I thought you were in a hurry."

Sevryn's right eyebrow twitched in a way that worried me for Etcher's life, but then Sevryn pinched the bridge of his nose and sighed. "Very well. Get to work." He gestured toward the bed with his free hand, then settled back down into the chair by the vanity.

Etcher moved toward the gold velvet curtains.

I glanced around, looking for a safe place to put Madison, and decided on a plush couch near the end of the bed. She would be close by if anything went wrong. I laid her down, made sure she looked comfortable enough, then hurried to join Etcher at the bed.

Etcher peeled the curtains apart and stuck his head through, then let out a low whistle. "He's in bad shape. I can see that right enough."

I peered over Etcher's hunched frame at the figure in the bed.

The man had thick, dark hair and a thick, dark beard flecked with grey. Judging by his jawline and broad shoulders, he may have been an imposing presence at one point, but now he looked wasted away. His skin—which should've been a rich, coppery-tan color—was sallow and pale. His cheeks were sunken in, and dark circles ringed his eyes. I could see the bones of his shoulders, and his collarbone jutted out. Sweat beaded his brow and jaw and had matted his curly hair, and though it wasn't hot in the room, his body let off a cloud of heat, like a fever. The thin, gold crown atop his head proved who he was—the treasonous king of Teionyr. *Beirthyr* himself.

I was tempted to kill him in his sleep, honor be hanged.

I couldn't. I knew I couldn't. But oh, how I wanted to.

Etcher seemed to pick up some of my anger. He glanced back at me over his shoulder. "Easy, young LeyGuard," he whispered. "There's a time to act, a time to observe, and a smart way to go about each of them. Understand?"

He held my eyes until I nodded. "Yes. I understand."

He breathed out and turned back around. "Good."

Etcher placed his hand on Beirthyr's sweaty forehead, then tipped Beirthyr's face from one side to the other, studying him. Then he stepped back, nearly knocking me over, and let the gold curtain swing shut behind us.

"Well?" Sevryn snapped from his chair.

Etcher turned to face him. "I can craft the rune to fix him, and this boy is strong enough to wield it. I can sense it in him. Not like the one you brought before."

The one he brought before? What did *that* mean?

Sevryn's glance bounced to me, and I thought I read a slight surprise there before he looked back at Etcher. "All right. And?"

"And nothing. I'll do it," Etcher said. "The one rune, and we're settled. Yes?"

Sevryn sighed. "So long as it *works*. That was our deal, I believe."

Etcher nodded. "Good."

Sevryn turned to me. "And you?"

I glanced at Etcher. "What do I have to do?"

"Just wield the rune I create. It will burn like a bugger, but it won't actually harm you. The trick will be holding your power steady long enough to channel the rune's full magic. It won't work if it's not properly wielded. But you've got the strength in you; I can see it. You'll do fine."

That didn't sound enjoyable—but for Ayla and Kaizyn's sake, not to mention Madison's and my own and now Etcher's, I supposed I had no choice but to try.

Sevryn stared me down. "Well? Are you going to be a thorn in my side, or does our agreement hold?"

I smirked at him. "Oh, it holds... *and* I'm going to be a thorn in your side. I'm an overachiever like that."

Etcher guffawed, but his laugh cut off short at a glare from Sevryn.

"Just get it done!" Sevryn snapped at Etcher. "How long do you need?"

Etcher shrugged. "Runing is a careful craft. I'll need three days, at least, to design it properly."

Sevryn narrowed his eyes, then sighed. "Very well, then. Three days. One hour longer, and it's both of your heads." He glanced at Madison. "And hers, as well."

"I quite like my head," Etcher muttered.

I stepped forward. "We'll get it done."

Sevryn studied me. "You'd better." He yanked open the door. "Guard! Return them to their chamber."

He spun back to Etcher as the guard headed our way. "You'll find all the usual Runing supplies waiting for you in your room. If there's anything additional you require, request it from the guard outside your room. But don't try to be clever—I'll know, if you're playing me."

Etcher nodded. "Yes, yes. But I'll need you to uncuff me so I can test the runes. You know it's a part of the process."

Sevryn stepped forward and touched a silver bracelet on his wrist to Etcher's cuff. Sevryn muttered a word under his voice, one I didn't catch, and Etcher's cuff popped open, then Sevryn handed the disengaged cuff to the guard... presumably for later use.

"The wards in the prison hall will prevent any fire magic," Sevryn told Etcher. "But with the cuff off, you should be able to access enough power to test your runes." He glared at me. "And don't you even *think* about asking for yours off. Etcher is too weak and old to be much trouble, but you—I'd sooner kill you than set you loose in this place. Your cuff will come off when it's time to wield the rune, and *only* then. And I'll be taking your *friend* as collateral when the time comes." He nodded at Madison.

I held his gaze. "Understood."

With that, Sevryn stormed out, and the guard from before swept in. "Follow me."

I hoisted Madison back onto my shoulder and hurried after the guard. Etcher once more trailed behind us.

I did trust my gut, and as I rolled back over the past few minutes in my head, I knew two things with certainty. One: the moment my truce with Sevryn was over, he was planning to kill me, regardless of what he'd said about returning me to my cell. And two: Etcher was not who he claimed to be.

# Chapter 10

# Until My Flame's Last Flickers Go Cold

*Striker*

Ayla stared at her smoking hand for a minute. It was actually vapor from the cold she'd exuded, not smoke, if I was correct—and I wouldn't have chucked a fireball at her if I hadn't been sure.

Then Ayla panicked. "No. No." She clenched her hands to her stomach, tucked right back up into a fetal position on the stone bench, and shook her head. "No, this doesn't make sense."

"Kid—" I began.

Her eyes cut to me with a tinge of anger—she was clearly still miffed that I'd tried to char her.

"Listen," I said, "Delayed magic like yours has happened before, okay? You only recently realized you had your grandfather's mind-gift, too, re-member? LeyGuard powers can activate at different times, and in different ways. For you, maybe coming into the Veil triggered it."

"Yeah... yeah, maybe," she muttered, but anyone could see she was still freaking out.

"She has the mind-gift?" Kaizyn asked, but Callan interjected before anyone could respond to that.

"*Ice* powers?" Callan turned his stare toward me. "That's not a usual LeyGuard manifestation, is it?"

Ayla flicked her head toward him. "*What?*"

I cut a glare at Callan. He wasn't wrong, but it hadn't been a helpful thing to say. The poor girl was freaked out enough already.

Prince Kaizyn stepped toward Ayla, and she seemed to calm a bit, like his presence soothed her. *Interesting.* How long had she been in here with him? Couldn't have been more than a few hours.

"Ayla." Kaizyn knelt in front of her and gently took one of her hands.

Ayla jumped a little, then looked up at him, like she hadn't noticed how close he was—her stare had still been on the fragments of melting ice scattered on the floor.

"Are you okay?" he asked.

The puppy-dog way he peered at her looked like a heap of trouble to me, but it seemed to wake Ayla from her trance.

She uncurled from her fetal position against the wall and sat up. "Yeah... I'm all right."

Callan and I shared a glance, then Callan stepped toward Ayla. "We'll talk about this and figure it out. But first... please don't panic, okay? We need to bring someone else inside."

Ayla slid forward on the seat, seeming more like her brave self by the minute. "Who?"

Callan winced. "Rory Kane."

I took that as my cue to slip back outside and lift Rory from where Vyrthil was guarding him, just outside the entrance where we'd had to set him down to fight off the beast we encountered.

Inside, I heard Ayla say, "*Rory*? He's here?"

Callan tried to prepare her for Rory's injuries, from what I could hear, but Ayla still gasped when I stepped back inside with him. I couldn't blame her; Rory looked terrible.

Kaizyn jumped into action at the sight of him, clearing a tangle of sheets from his mattress in the corner. "Put him here."

I glanced at Callan, and he nodded.

Callan had explained on the way over that Prince Kaizyn had trained as a healer. Callan had too, to an extent, but apparently Kaizyn had been something of a prodigy at it. He didn't have magic healing ability, but he had some basic faespell serums, and he knew how to treat injuries.

I'd have preferred a full LeyGuard med-lab, but this cave Kaizyn lived in was also the only safe place to hide within two days' walk inside the Veil. Beggars couldn't be choosers. Especially when someone was bleeding to death.

I set Rory carefully on the mattress, then stepped back.

Kaizyn immediately went to work, peeling loose our makeshift bandage to take a better look.

Ayla hovered behind him, chewing nervously on a fingernail. "How bad is it?"

Kaizyn glanced back at her. "Bad," he said plainly, and I was impressed he hadn't tried to sugar-coat it. "Grab me two of the red vials from the shelf, the roll of cloth, and one of the purple vials."

Ayla dashed off to find what he asked for.

Callan stepped close to me. "It was an act of deep trust and desperation, bringing you here," he said in a low voice.

I kept my voice low to match his. "I'm aware."

"No one can know where the prince is."

I turned to look at him. "Do you think I'm dense? Of course not."

Callan looked like he wanted to retort, but he took a deep breath and held my gaze. "I cannot be the reason he gets found."

I met his gaze in return. "Neither can I." I glanced at Ayla, who was busy opening and holding vials for Kaizyn as he tended Rory's wound. Then I turned back to Callan. "Listen—I'm responsible for that girl over there. I owe her grandfather, and more than that, I made her a promise. Her life is tied to the prince's life, right? And I keep my promises. I'll protect the both of them until they're both safe or until my flame's last flickers go cold. Won't you?"

Callan's jaw tightened, and he gave me a curt nod. "Until they're safe, or my flame's last flickers go cold."

"Good." I chewed on my match and grinned. "Then I suppose I won't have to kill you."

Callan laughed, but it cut short as Ayla called for us.

"Striker? Callan?" Her voice carried a thread of fear.

We both turned toward her.

Kaizyn stood, wiping blood from his hands onto a dark towel. "He's stable for now, but that won't last. One side of the wound is deep. It barely missed his spine and organs, and I suspect he's also bleeding internally. He needs more care than I can give. Runestones, like the LeyGuards have, might be enough. Or more powerful faespells. But with what I have here..." His eyes were wide and distraught. "I've done my best, but if he stays here, there's a good chance he won't survive."

Callan tensed.

"There's no LeyGuard outpost within two days' walk," I said.

Callan turned to Kaizyn. "Will he make it that far?"

Kaizyn shook his head. "I don't think so. The damage is critical as is; the travel would only worsen it."

Ayla glanced between the three of us. "Isn't there *something* you can do? We can't just let him die!"

There was an anguish on her face, something personal—almost like she blamed herself.

Kaizyn stared at her, mirroring her grief on his face as though he felt it too, though five minutes earlier he probably couldn't have told Rory apart from the first Adam.

I stepped toward Ayla. "Kid, listen. It's not your—"

Kaizyn spun toward Callan. "I know where we can take him."

Callan and Kaizyn stared at each other for a moment. "There's no place anywhere close we can trust," Callan said. "There are no allies in any realm that touches this part of the... Veil..." His speech trailed off as he seemed to realize something, then he clenched his jaw. "They'll never let us in."

Kaizyn stepped toward him. "They'll let *me* in."

"You can't leave the Veil!"

"It overlaps with the Veil's edge. I can't go all the way in, but I can go with you to the doorway. They'll help us if I'm there. You know they will."

Callan shook his head. "It's too risky. If anyone finds out where you're hiding—"

Kaizyn glanced at Ayla, who was clutching Rory's pale hand, then turned to Callan. "I have to do this. Let me help." He straightened his spine. "My father is gone, now. I'm your *king*."

Callan gawked at Kaizyn for a moment and opened his mouth like he was about to argue—then simply closed his mouth and bowed. "As you wish."

I'd had enough of their cryptic exchange. I stepped forward. "Mind telling the rest of us what you two decided *we're* all going to do?"

Kaizyn turned toward me and gave me a respectful nod. "I would never require any of you to accompany me where we are headed. I can do this alone, if needed—though it would help to have someone bigger, like you, to carry the injured human. The faster we can move, the better. In fact, it may be best if it were only you and me."

Callan stiffened. "You can't go without my protection, Kaizyn. As the head of your guard—"

"You're my *only* remaining guard," Kaizyn muttered.

"All the more, then," Callan said, his eyes hard. "If you insist on this, I'm going with you."

Ayla stood, still clutching Rory's hand. "Well, if you're all going, I'm going, too. I'm not staying here alone."

Callan sighed and muttered some choice Fae curses.

I ran a hand over my face. "Fine. It's a party. But where, exactly, are we going?"

Kaizyn turned toward me. "Arcvale."

I gaped at him. "*Arcvale*? Wasn't that place destroyed in a Dark Fae incursion nearly twenty years ago and abandoned by all the ArcFae?"

Brone and I hadn't been a part of that battalion, but the LeyGuards who helped the ArcFae escape said they were powerful, that they possessed strange magic... but they'd been betrayed by one of their own, then overwhelmed by a swarm of Dark Fae minions. Most of the ArcFae died in the attack while our Guards were trying to open a LeyGate for them to flee Earthside.

I shook my head at the Fae prince. "I heard darklings swarmed the whole dome. The Dark Fae have controlled it ever since. We'll never get inside, even if there was anything still there worth getting inside *for.*"

"Not *everyone* fled." Kaizyn gave me a devious smile. "And I know the way in."

# CHAPTER 11

# WITH YOU, THAT'S IMPOSSIBLE

*Ayla*

Wandering the Veil again didn't thrill me, but at least I wasn't alone this time.

Both Striker and Callan had cast small orbs with their fire magic which hovered on either side of our group to give light as we walked. The magic glowed reddish for Striker's and more orange for Callan's—LeyGuard fire magic and fire-Fae magic were similar, but not identical.

Callan took the lead, scouting our way through the darkness. He knew where this mysterious door to Arcvale was, though he still didn't seem happy we were going.

Striker took up the rear, wearing a backpack of supplies and carrying Rory as though he weighed nothing. He'd returned the lighter pack to me.

Vyrthil stalked on Striker's heels, ears flicking as he listened for approaching monsters.

Kaizyn walked by my side in the middle, quiet but close, as though trying to reassure me with his presence.

Surprisingly, it was working. Being near him made me feel calm... unlike the discovery that I might have ice magic. *That* made me want to freak out, though I was doing my best to hold it together for now, for Rory's sake. I kept telling myself I could have my meltdown later, not that it was helping much.

Kaizyn glanced over at me. "Your friend, or your magic?" he asked softly.

It took me a moment to realize he was asking where my panicked feelings were coming from. Because, of course, he felt them too.

I drew a shaky breath, which turned into a nervous laugh. "Both, I guess?" I *was* worried about Rory, and I felt selfish for letting concerns about my potential magic overshadow his serious injuries, but—good gravy, I was worried about the magic, too. I couldn't have magic. I didn't *want* magic.

Sure, I knew plenty of kids would give anything to have the magic they read about in storybooks. But here in the Veil, surrounded by monsters and Dark Fae who wanted to *kill* me to get to Kaizyn, magic felt like a liability—just another reason for someone to want me dead.

If I'd trained from birth as a LeyGuard, I was sure it would be different. I would know how to use my magic, how to protect myself and others with it. But puffs of frost? Shattering ice-air? I didn't understand my magic and had no *control* over it, which only made it a risk for me and everyone else. Unless... I could learn?

Kaizyn turned to look at me again. "Something shifted in you. Curiosity? Resolve?"

I met his gaze. "I thought you said you would try not to read my feelings."

His tanned skin flushed. "I apologize. I just... It is hard to block them out, especially when I—when I am worried about you." The last words came out in a rush. He broke eye contact, looking off to the side.

He hadn't asked for this strange bond, either. He'd been dying, and I wasn't even the one he'd meant to bond with.

I sighed. "It's all right. I'm just not used to talking so much about my feelings. I like to keep my thoughts private. But with you, that's impossible."

His gaze slid to mine for a second, then away again. "I'm sorry."

I sighed again. "It's fine."

It might have made me feel a little better if I could read Kaizyn's feelings, too, rather than the vague sensations I got through my side of the bond. Perhaps if it were mutual, I wouldn't feel so exposed.

I glanced behind me. If Striker had heard our awkward exchange, he gave no sign of it. And Callan, in front of us, was focused on navigating our path. Well, at least there was that. I hadn't laid my emotions bare for *everyone*; Kaizyn had kept his voice low enough to ensure that. At least he was considerate.

We walked along in silence.

After a few more moments, Kaizyn spoke again, his voice still soft. "Could we talk about something? Not what you're feeling. Something else."

I got that clenched feeling in my chest that surfaced every time someone said a variation of *We need to talk*, but I shoved it away and shrugged. "Yeah, sure." I didn't know if he had a topic in mind or just wanted to chat. Either way, the expectation for awkward conversations with Kaizyn had been firmly established, and I doubted things could get much worse. "What do you want to talk about?"

Kaizyn gestured at the pack I carried. "Callan mentioned you had a journal of your grandfather's, something with his notes in it. Did you bring it with you?"

His question took me by surprise, because to be honest, I'd almost forgotten Striker and I had packed it in one bag. "Yeah, I think I did. I'm not sure if it's in Striker's pack or mine."

Kaizyn cut his eyes to me, almost hesitantly. "Can I... see it? If you have it?"

I nearly said *no*. My grandfather's journal was the only resource I had for figuring out the true name, plus how to break Kaizyn's curse and maybe even our bond.

But then I realized no one was more directly impacted by all of that—besides myself, of course—than Kaizyn. It seemed selfish *not* to let him see it.

"Uh... sure," I said. I slid the pack off one arm and swung it forward so I could open it and look inside.

True to my nature, I stumbled over my own feet the moment I took my eyes off where I was walking.

Kaizyn steadied me with a hand on my arm, but he pulled it away as soon as I got my balance.

"Thanks," I muttered, embarrassed I was so clumsy.

His answer came softly. "Of course."

It turned out my grandfather's journal *was* in my pack, along with some rope and bandages and other things. I slid it out, and my heart lurched at the familiar feel of it, the smooth leather, the metallic etchings. It was my grandfather's *life* in here—his words, his thoughts—a tiny piece of home. Images of Grandpa in the hospital at the Hub and Mom and Dad in their Selkblood comas rushed in at me, squeezing my heart so hard it hurt.

I forced a breath, then handed the journal to Kaizyn so I could zip up the pack and return it to my back.

His touch was reverent as he took the journal. His eyes slid up to mine. "Thank you for trusting me with it."

Because, of course, he could feel what it meant to me. Good gravy, that was still awkward. I supposed it wasn't a *bad* thing to have a friend who understood you the way Kaizyn understood me. But in this case, that understanding came with unrequited feelings on his side and an implied betrothal, so... that part wasn't great. I could try not to be so weirded out by it, though, for his sake. I wanted to be friends.

Kaizyn opened the journal and flipped through it as we walked. He seemed to have no problem reading and walking, but he was Fae and moved with a tense, panther-like grace.

I was clumsy and always had been.

"It could be in here somewhere." Kaizyn slowly turned the pages. "My true name, the thing that could break the Teionyr Seal." He chuckled darkly, then glanced at me. "Isn't it strange that the very thing that could break this curse may also be what removes the Seal that prevented my uncle from killing me?" His gaze hardened. "If Beirthyr finds the name—or realizes I've found it and used it to free myself—he *will* try again."

"We won't let that happen," Striker's deep voice said from behind us.

So he *had* been listening, at least to that part.

Kaizyn nodded. "I am grateful for your protection. All the same, it feels odd to hold this in my hand, knowing what it might contain." He looked over at me again. "I would like to sit down and look at this more carefully later, if it's okay with you." He closed the journal and handed it back to me.

I clutched it to my chest and nodded. "Of course."

We walked in silence for a few more moments, then Kaizyn said, "Before the power you manifested today, I was not aware you had awakened any of your LeyGuard magic yet."

*Yet.* I remembered Callan had said that Kaizyn could feel my latent magic through the bond, along with everything else he felt. Could he feel *what* magic I had the potential to develop, or just a sense that I had LeyGuard magic in me somewhere? I was afraid to ask… but Kaizyn seemed surprised by whatever that crazy ice thing was I'd done, so I doubted he knew anything specific about what I could do.

Kaizyn glanced at me, his eyes bright with curiosity. "Is the mind-gift Striker mentioned the only other magic you've manifested besides the power you used in the cave?"

I wasn't sure I would call randomly freezing things a *power*, especially when I couldn't control it, but I nodded. "Yeah, just those two… so far." I laughed awkwardly.

"Would it be all right if I asked what your mind-gift does? I've heard your grandfather had it, but I'm not very familiar with what that particular LeyGuard ability includes."

"Oh, no, that's fine." I shrugged. "It's… kind of like communicating with my mind, like hearing others' thoughts in my head."

Kaizyn gasped. "Is that rare among LeyGuard? Magic like that is rare among the Fae. Legends say one of my ancestors could do something similar, communicate by sending and receiving messages with his mind across distances. It was tied to his sear-bind, somehow." He smiled. "He bonded with a dragon—the first and only time a Teionyrian royal has ever summoned a sear-bind that powerful. A dragon is the rarest creature of the Wilds there is. We aren't sure any more are still alive, but my father would have given *anything* to have a dragon on our side in this war." He turned to look at me. "If you possess magic like that, you must be more powerful than you realize."

I shook my head. "I think the mind-gift might be rare for LeyGuards, but mine isn't like what you described. It's one-way, from what I can tell. I'm just the receiver, and other people can kind of yell at me. In my brain. At least, they can if I know them well enough, so that I recognize their frequency or something. I'm not even sure how it works."

Kaizyn's eyes widened. "That seems... useful?"

I laughed at his politeness. "You mean 'irritating.'" I smiled at him. "But yes, also useful, sometimes. Callan and Jordan were both able to communicate with me in my mind to warn me, or to ask questions without others hearing. With Jordan, it saved my life." Longing slammed hard into my chest as I thought back to the day Jordan burst through my grandfather's window with his dagger and his armored dog. *Good heavens,* I missed him, and it *hurt.*

Kaizyn placed a hand on my arm.

I almost pulled away, but his expression was so tender and concerned, I stopped myself. His touch *was* comforting, like a... well, like a friend.

"We will find him, Ayla," he said.

And somehow it helped. I gave him a weak smile. "Thanks."

Callan stopped so suddenly I nearly ran into him.

He glanced back over his shoulder. "We're here."

Kaizyn squeezed my arm, then stepped up next to Callan.

Kaizyn stretched out his hand, and his fingers surged bright with a golden glow as he channeled his magic.

The air in front of him shimmered, then a door appeared. Just an ordinary wooden door with a brass knob, like the door to a bedroom, floating in the middle of the blackness.

Kaizyn paused a moment, panting, then reached for the doorknob.

Callan grabbed Kaizyn's arm. "I'm begging you one last time—don't do this. It's too big of a risk."

Kaizyn looked past me, at Rory sagging in Striker's arms, then turned back to Callan. "The decision has already been made."

Alarm flared in my chest as I glanced between them. An unspoken tension hung between their words, and I couldn't help but feel this door involved danger they hadn't explained to us.

"Wait—what risk?" I asked. "You mean just that they might figure out where Kaizyn is hiding, right? Or that they might tell someone else he's here?"

Kaizyn glanced back at me. "It's all right, Ayla." He turned to Callan. "You'll protect her? If—"

"Of course." Callan's hand moved to his knife.

Before I could ask what he meant, Kaizyn yanked open the door—then collapsed to his knees with a gut-wrenching shout of pain.

# CHAPTER 12

# ALL MAGIC HAS A COST

*Ayla*

I rushed toward Kaizyn and dropped to my knees next to him.

He collapsed onto his side, his trembling body summoning memories of the night we'd first met.

"Kaizyn!" I spun to Callan. "What's happening to him?" I shouted. "Do something!"

Callan clenched his jaw, his eyes locked on Kaizyn.

But then Kaizyn sucked a long breath, and his trembling stilled. He moaned and slowly sat up.

I reached for him by instinct, steadying him as he got his bearings.

Callan rushed to Kaizyn's side by the door, which now hung slightly ajar. "Is it over?"

Something like sunlight spilled through the thin opening of the door beside him, shockingly bright in all the surrounding darkness.

Kaizyn's answer came breathlessly: "Yes. I told you I was strong enough."

Callan rolled his eyes. "I believed you, but it was still a stupid risk to take."

I stared between the two of them. "What *was* that? Kaizyn, are you okay?"

Callan helped him to his feet, and though Kaizyn tried to cover it, his legs nearly gave out as he stood.

Callan glanced at me. "The doorway requires an offering—a siphoning of life-magic."

I gaped at him, then at Kaizyn. "You mean... you just siphoned away years of your life or something?!" I couldn't help but think of the machine from *The Princess Bride.*

Kaizyn laughed, then winced and grabbed his side. He was obviously still sore. "No, no years off my life. Just a sharp—and painful—draining of my energy. I'll recover. Though if this door did that to someone whose innate magic wasn't strong enough, it could be deadly."

I stared at him. "Why—why would you risk that?"

I understood, now, why Callan had been so against it.

Striker shifted Rory in his arms and grunted, leveling a glare at Kaizyn. "I'm wondering the same thing."

"We need their help for your friend," Kaizyn said.

His deep blue eyes locked on mine, steady. "All magic has a cost, Ayla. That was mine, for opening the door. I'm okay. Really. I've been here before; I knew what would happen. There was a risk I might fall unconscious, but I would not have done it if I didn't know for certain I could manage any strain beyond that. Risking *my* life would have also put you at risk, and that I would *never* do." A soft laugh escaped him as he clenched his side again. "Not that it didn't hurt."

He stepped back, then glanced at the door. "We should get your friend inside, but I'll need to speak to them first, to make arrangements for you all to enter."

*Right*—he couldn't leave the Veil. Whatever this place beyond the door was, it must be actually in Faeside, not in the strange in-between where we'd traveled so far.

Kaizyn's gaze held mine, and I could see that he was fine; his strength was returning. But my chest clenched at the thought that we were going for help from someone who required crippling pain and a sacrifice of *life energy* just for coming here.

I glanced at the silver of light from the open door. "Are you sure this is safe?"

Kaizyn nodded. "Once I speak with them, yes. But if I have any doubts after talking with them, we'll leave. Don't worry; it will all be fine."

I tensed as Kaizyn's hand closed over the doorknob again, but this time nothing bad happened.

He pulled open the door.

The sliver of sunlight widened, revealing what looked like a blue sky and a sprawling, grass field beyond the opening, with rows of tall, wispy, wheat-like crops over to one side and the cluster of small, stone-shingled buildings visible in the distance. A village?

A woman stepped into view, maybe a few years older than me. She was beautiful, with large, dark eyes and dusky skin, and slim in a way that betrayed lithe strength. She wore a simple, dark brown dress with flowing sleeves—and she had *wings*. Long, black, featherless wings that arched up over the top of her shoulders and swept down to dust the ground behind her, like the wings on drawings of dragons in fairytale books. Long, flowing hair cascaded around her shoulders and down her sides in a startling shade of white-blond that reminded me of lightning. And below her clavicle, just above the squared neckline of her dress, there was a crackling, bright-white circle, like someone had embedded a ball of electricity in her chest.

I realized I was gaping and averted my eyes back to her face, hoping I hadn't offended her.

But her gaze wasn't on me. She was looking at Kaizyn.

"I told you not to bring others here." Her voice was calm, almost musical, but her dark eyes were hard.

Kaizyn stepped forward and tipped his head in a slight bow.

Who *was* this woman, if even a prince bowed to her? Was she a royal, too?

"'Dame Keyja," Kaizyn said with a tone of respect, then straightened from his bow to meet her glare, though he offered no explanation for our presence.

Keyja swept her eyes over the rest of us, evaluating.

I stood still, following Callan and Kaizyn's lead.

I was getting nervous at the extended silence, but then Keyja's gaze caught on Rory in Striker's arms, and her eyes widened. "Someone is hurt." There was a thread of concern in her voice.

Kaizyn nodded. "Yes."

Keyja's eyes slid back to Kaizyn. "This is why you have come?"

Kaizyn held her stare. "Yes."

"You are still cursed. You cannot enter."

I startled at the stark way she said that. Apparently, Kaizyn's curse was no secret to this woman.

He gave a slight nod. "Yes. And no, I cannot."

Keyja studied him a moment longer, then her eyes softened, and she sighed. Her shoulders relaxed and her wings lifted slightly. "Very well. I will honor our friendship. But you know that if you expose us—"

Kaizyn shook his head. "These friends are trustworthy. I vouch for them with my life."

Keyja tipped her head. "Indeed. You do." She stepped back and swept her arm wide, like an invitation. "Come, new friends. You may enter."

Callan hung back next to Kaizyn. "I don't feel right leaving you again."

Kaizyn narrowed his eyes. "You made me a promise."

"Yes, but that was Earthside. Things here are—"

"Nothing has changed," Kaizyn interrupted.

Callan glanced at me, making me wonder suddenly if this cryptic argument was about *me.*

"Nothing has changed," Kaizyn said again, his tone firmer this time.

Callan and Kaizyn shared a wordless exchange of glares, but apparently Kaizyn won their staring argument, because Callan sighed and nodded.

"Fine. But don't do anything else that's reckless while I'm gone." Callan swept past me, then waved for Striker to follow him with Rory.

I hesitated, unsettled by the sudden shift in this woman's demeanor... and by her wings... and the glowing orb in her chest... and the punishing pain-doorknob... basically, by the whole situation.

Kaizyn stepped close beside me. "I feel your fear," he whispered. "But you will be safe here. Keyja and the two others who live here are friends."

I huffed a breathless laugh. "Could've fooled me."

But I relaxed slightly at the knowledge that there were only three people who lived inside this place. Worst-case scenario, Striker and Callan could take three dragon-winged, glowing-orb-chested people... couldn't they?

Kaizyn stepped back, then gestured at the doorway. "Go on. Keyja's mother was a skilled apothecarist. There are faespells here that can help your friend."

Vyrthil sidled up next to him, glowing a faint orange.

Though I wanted to stay close to Striker and Rory, I was reluctant to leave Kaizyn alone out here in the darkness. "But where will *you* go? You'll be alone."

Kaizyn smiled gently. "I have grown accustomed to being alone, Ayla Rogers. Besides, I have Vyrthil. Now, go. Be there for your friend."

I stepped toward the door, still feeling torn as I stared at the welcoming landscape and the cheerful blue sky. I really should go with Rory. Surely Kaizyn would be okay alone, for a bit. He'd already been hiding on his own in the Veil for a while. Still, the thought of him going back to a dark, lonely cave or hiding out in this bleak expanse of darkness while the rest of us stepped into this sunlit village just made me... sad. But Madison and I had grown close the past few days, and Rory was her brother. If our roles had been reversed, staying with my injured family member to make sure he was okay was what I would've hoped for Madison to do. So it was what I needed to do now, too.

When I looked back to say goodbye to Kaizyn, he was already gone.

I turned forward and stepped through the doorway.

# CHAPTER 13

# EVER HEARD OF MADDOX ROGERS?

*Jordan*

The guard gestured Etcher and me into our room and slammed the door behind us. I heard the lock engage as I turned to set Madison on the bed.

The overhead light from earlier was still on, illuminating a pile of Runing supplies someone had shoved in with the hanging shirts in the now-open armoire: fountain pens, parchment, and two small tubs of ink—a plain, black ink for practice and an opalescent, charcoal ink I recognized as the ink for etching semi-permanent runes onto skin. There were no tattooing supplies like permanent runes required, but our task with Beirthyr didn't call for that sort of rune. Someone had also placed a small, wooden table next to Etcher's bed, I assumed for use as a work surface.

Etcher shuffled over to the armoire and began sorting the supplies onto the table.

I watched him for a moment, my suspicions coalescing into certainty. "You aren't Etcher."

His hands stilled. He glanced at me over his shoulder. "What? Of course I am."

I stepped toward him, itching for the dagger the Fae guards had taken from me. "You told Sevryn you needed your ward-cuffs off so you could test the runes. The books say Etcher never tested his runes. It was a point of pride for him; he could tell exactly what a rune would do just by looking at it."

Etcher released the fountain pen he'd been holding, letting it clatter to the table. He turned around slowly. His dark eyes met mine with an unreadable intensity. "Maybe I've grown more cautious in my old age."

"Or maybe you're not Etcher at all."

I held his firm gaze.

Finally, he sighed. "Fine, kid. You got me. You gonna turn me in?"

"To Sevryn? Of course not."

He narrowed his eyes at me. "Then what's your point?"

I crossed my arms. "If you expect me to wield this rune for you, you owe me the truth: who you are, and what you're up to here—*really*." My gut still said I could trust him, but he'd already lied to me at least once, and I wasn't planning to take any chances.

His perceptive gaze studied me for a moment longer, then he nodded and held out his hand. "Tharin Davis. I *am* a Valos Runist, and I didn't completely lie—my friends at the Hub called me Etcher. A nickname, after the real one, because of my talents... if he ever actually existed. I've always wondered if he was just a myth."

I tentatively shook his hand, though my guard was still up. "Fine... Tharin." I dropped my hand, and yet again it itched for my missing dagger.

He shrugged. "Well, since I'm not upholding *that* ruse, anymore..." He tapped the rune on his arm, and the wrinkled, stooped, old man transformed right in front of me into a weathered, muscular man about my height, with dark hair and dark eyes, a few years older than my own parents.

I gaped at him. "Why—*what*? I thought you said that was a long-life rune!"

He grinned. "Disguise rune. An original design, and I'm rather proud of it. I can only shift with it when my magic is free, though." He rolled his neck and shoulders. "Ah, it feels good to be young again, even if I can only risk my true form for a few moments." He arched his back in a long stretch, then sighed and tapped the rune again. He transformed back into the old man before my eyes, then shrugged. "I've invested way too much in this to risk getting caught now."

His nonchalance and partial answers rubbed me the wrong way—or maybe I was just irked that I'd fallen for his tricks. "Why *are* you here, Tharin? Were you really captured, like you said?" Disguise was a common strategy for infiltration, though; it didn't *necessarily* mean I couldn't trust him.

"Of course. I wouldn't be here by choice. May as well do what I can to end this war while I'm here, though, right?" He turned back to organizing the supplies, though he glanced at me as he talked. "And call me Etcher, still. It's better to avoid a slip-up, and I'm used to answering to it, anyway."

I scanned his body language, looking for signs of deception, but found nothing. My instincts for that were *usually* pretty good. I felt myself swaying back toward trusting him, but I had to be sure. "Why lie about who you are?"

"The less they know about me, the more I can accomplish. Turns out, old men aren't high on the suspicion scale. Now that I've lived a couple decades with these creaky knees and bad back, I can understand why."

"But you've *helped* them, right? You've helped Sevryn?"

Tharin—Etcher, as he'd told me to keep calling him—met my gaze. "Have I?"

"You said he'd brought you someone to wield runes before, and... you seemed to have a deal with Sevryn."

"A deal I've yet to fulfill my part of. I've been here since long before Sevryn, but I wasn't about to leave once he arrived. Not when I could be of use."

I supposed he had a point. Maybe he'd only *pretended* to help Sevryn.

Etcher sighed. "Look, kid, I don't have to explain myself to you. But if it gives you peace of mind, I'm loyal to the *actual* king of Teionyr—who, now that King Veilar is dead, is his son. That's the only reason I've kept this ruse up for so long."

A tiny spark of hope flared in my chest. "You're here for Kaizyn?"

"I'm here to destroy Beirthyr and Sevryn... and then I'm getting *you* out of here." He straightened the stack of parchment on the table, then turned to me. "This is no place for a LeyGuard kid."

I narrowed my eyes. "You said you were captured *decades* ago. That means the Teionyrians imprisoned you long before Sevryn showed up. LeyGuards are supposed to be *allies* to Teionyr. Why would they have kept you here?"

He glanced up at me. "Let's just say I made certain that they would. I needed to be here, to monitor things. I haven't always been a prisoner, but it has its uses. And I don't consider myself LeyGuard anymore—not really. I don't trust the Hub as far as I could throw it, which, given that it's a massive complex tucked inside a Ley-pocket, is no distance at all. I'm here for my own purposes."

That unsettled me. "Why *are* you here, then?"

He picked up an empty fountain pen and ran his thumb carefully over its sharp tip. His wrinkled skin looked so thin, I worried the pen might cut him, but apparently his skin was tougher than it looked. He stroked his thumb over the sharp pen tip, back and forth, staring at it. "Ever heard of Maddox Rogers?"

My heart tripped in my chest. *Ayla's grandfather?* I did my best to keep my expression calm as I answered. "Yes. I've met him."

He looked up, assessing my face. "Met him *how*? Through the Hub?"

A dark chuckle escaped me. "Not exactly. He's my... friend's grandfather." I'd nearly said *girlfriend*, but Ayla and I hadn't exactly had time to define things before I'd gotten dragged off into this mess.

Etcher stiffened. "None of Maddox's family was supposed to know he was LeyGuard."

I blinked at him, a bit startled by his response. "They didn't. I'm not even sure *Maddox* knew, anymore. At least, not until Sevryn went after him a few weeks ago."

Etcher studied me and seemed to decide he could trust me. The wall behind his expression came down. "I was here when Maddox Rogers rescued the infant prince," he said. "I was one of the LeyGuards on his team. I was young but loyal to Maddox, and to our cause. Since then, I have done everything I could to protect the royal family. You'd be surprised how much leeway you can get, even as a prisoner, when they think you're a fragile old man." He held up his wrists, showing his lack of rune-cuffs. "It just wasn't enough."

I stepped toward him. "We pulled our forces out of Upper Faeside over a decade ago. If your team knew you were still in Teionyr, why would they have *left* you here? The LeyGuard—"

"Doesn't abandon its own?" He shrugged. "Like I said, they probably think I'm dead." He looked down. "There were many who died that day. Plus, as I *also* said, I stayed here to make sure the royals were protected." He ran his thumb over the pen's tip again, then looked up at me, and his expression had changed to resolve. "Maybe I'm not the real Etcher—if he ever really existed—but I know my runes, and I'm getting you out of here."

"You keep saying that you're gonna take out Beirthyr and Sevryn, and get *me* out of here." I stilled, watching him. "You don't say it like you're coming with me."

He ran a wrinkled hand down his face. "I still have business here." He paused. "Something I owe Maddox."

How was *everything* related to helping Ayla and her grandfather? But I supposed the Rogers family were just that way—they inspired deep loyalty.

I swallowed. "About that... Maddox's granddaughter, Ayla, might be trapped somewhere in Faeside."

Etcher's face flicked up at me in surprise.

I straightened my shoulders. "I'm not going back Earthside without her."

Etcher tipped his head, studying me. "You're *involved* with Maddox's granddaughter?"

I supposed my concern for her was obvious. I nodded. "You could say that."

Etcher cursed in a language I'd never heard before—but I certainly understood the tone.

"What?" I asked.

Etcher sighed and met my stare. "This just got more complicated. Saving some girl wasn't the plan."

"You said you were loyal to Maddox. Don't you think he'd want his granddaughter saved? You just said you owed him!"

Etcher glared at me. "… I suppose I did."

Suspicion flared within me, that gut-deep instinct I'd learned not to ignore. I narrowed my eyes. "What aren't you telling me?"

He held his glare a moment longer, then his face softened. "I can't tell you, yet. I just need you to trust me."

I threw my hands up. "How am I supposed to trust you when you say something like *that*?"

He squared himself to face me, though his posture was calm, rather than threatening.

His gaze held mine. "What does your gut say?"

I stared at him for a moment, then sighed. "To trust you."

And it did… despite all logic to the contrary.

# CHAPTER 14

# IT WOULD DESTROY ME

*Jordan*

Etcher relaxed and nodded. "I'm on your side. That's all you need to know. Now, let's craft ourselves a rune that can take down a false king *and* the snake controlling him." He spun back toward the table.

"Controlling him." I thought back to my conversations with Sevryn, and what I knew Selkbloods were capable of. The Hub thought Beirthyr had actively usurped the throne and invited the Selkbloods in, but... "Did you mean that literally?"

Etcher glanced at me. "Didn't you notice Sevryn was sitting at the king's desk when we entered his chambers? He had a stamp and a folded letter in his hand. He stuffed them away when we came in, but my guess is that Sevryn is sending missives out as though he's the king." Etcher slid a sheet of parchment from the stack and opened the well of practice ink. "No one in the palace knows Beirthyr is unconscious except Sevryn, and now us. Perhaps Beirthyr never really *was* fully conscious—he could've been operating under Selkblood mind-control for this entire coup. His sear-bind turning on him may not have been an accident; it could all be part of Sevryn's plan to eliminate Beirthyr and take control of Teionyr himself."

I pondered that for a moment. "Sevryn really seemed to want Beirthyr alive. Why go through all this and have us craft a rune to save him, if he's just planning to get rid of him and take over his kingdom?" This same question had plagued me from the moment Sevryn and I first made our deal.

Etcher shrugged. "Maybe he needs him as a figurehead, to keep up appearances. Or maybe Beirthyr's sear-bind was trying to *help* Beirthyr by fighting off Sevryn's control with its fire magic, and Sevryn wants our rune to sever the sear-bind and finish the job."

My heart lurched. "Is that possible? You mean Beirthyr could be in something like a Selkblood coma, under Sevryn's control, but fighting him?"

Thoughts of Ayla's parents flashed in, of how helpless they'd looked when we found them. I hoped the Hub had been able to help them. If not, Ayla would be devastated—*Ayla*. I didn't even know where she *was* now. I could only pray she was okay.

Etcher shrugged again. "I suppose it's possible. I won't know for sure until after we apply the runes."

"Until *after* we apply the runes?" I shook my head. "But you're crafting runes that will take both of them out, right? It's not really meant to help him?"

He stared at me. "Of course."

"If Beirthyr is trying to *fight* Sevryn, if he's innocent..."

Etcher interrupted me. "Beirthyr is *not* the rightful king. Even if he didn't *choose* this, he does not belong on that throne."

"That doesn't mean we can murder him!"

Etcher glared at me, then sighed. "Even if he's innocent, he may be too far gone, already. And in the end, he *let* the Dark Fae into the city. He's the one who struck up the friendship with Sevryn in the first place, trying to arrange some kind of behind-the-scenes trade deal right under King Veilar's nose. Even if I were to save him, we can't trust him. Whether he knew the Selkblood's true intentions or not, he invited them in."

I clenched my jaw. The thought of killing Beirthyr before we truly knew his part in this just didn't sit well with me. "So maybe we can't trust him. That doesn't justify *killing* him. People make mistakes. And the Selkbloods could've been manipulating him, even back then."

Etcher stiffened and studied me for several long, tense moments. Then his shoulders sagged, and he relented. "Okay, boy. Your gut says mercy, mercy it is. If I sense he's being controlled when I apply the runes, we can try to save him." He brandished a fountain pen like a tiny sword and pointed it at me. "But we're not letting him go free. If we pull this off, Beirthyr goes straight to the dungeons."

He'd changed his mind and decided not to fight me on this. I wasn't sure why, but I'd take my good luck where I could. I nodded. "Agreed." I glanced at Madison. "But if you're getting me out of here, she comes, too."

Etcher rolled his eyes. "Of course. I'm a shady old man, not a heartless fiend."

I scanned his face, but he looked genuine. "Right. Okay... good."

"Are you done now? What about Sevryn? You gonna insist we save him, too?" Etcher punctuated each word by jabbing the fountain pen in the air for emphasis.

I was a little worried he might actually stab me with it.

"Sevryn has hurt people I love," I said, "and he'd gladly do it again. Also, I'm pretty sure he's planning to kill me."

Etcher's eyes widened slightly. "Well, we can't let *that* happen."

"We can't let him escape," I continued. "He needs to pay for what he's done. But this isn't our kingdom, and we're not executioners. The LeyGuard has always let the Fae apply their own systems of justice, unless lives are directly at stake."

Etcher tapped the pen against his opposite palm. "So, then..." He looked at me expectantly.

"We capture him, if we can. Let the rightful king decide what to do with him."

I doubted there were many scenarios where Madison and I escaped that didn't involve at least incapacitating Sevryn, if not worse... but that didn't necessarily mean we needed to *kill* him. I might loathe Sevryn, but

I wouldn't let my anger toward him bend my principles. Teionyr had laws, and so did the LeyGuard. We needed to do this right.

"And if we can't? If lives *are* directly at stake?"

I met his gaze with all the anger I felt for what Sevryn had done. "Then we do what we have to."

Etcher grinned. "*That*"—he flourished the fountain pen for emphasis—"I can get on board with."

I smiled back at him, but my smile didn't hold long.

"Sevryn isn't our only problem, though," I said. "He's got an entire team of Selkbloods working with him. I saw some of them Earthside. And he seems to have replaced some of the palace guards with his own personal mercenaries—I talked to one in the dungeon. They're loyal to him. Taking Sevryn down, and maybe even Beirthyr, won't be enough. We'll need a rune that will disable *all* of them somehow."

"Oh, I'm *very* aware of all that. I've been here a long time, remember?" Etcher leaned toward me. "I may not leave this room much, but I hear things. There are a half-dozen Selkbloods in this palace. Some of the current guards are hired in like you said, and the rest of them have joined Sevryn's side—willingly or not, I can't say. The guards who remained loyal to King Veilar were killed or imprisoned weeks ago."

That saddened me—and surprised me. "There are guards in the prison who are loyal to Veilar? I didn't see anyone else down there."

Etcher shook his head. "You wouldn't have; they aren't kept here in the palace. Sevryn had them moved to the barracks north of the market square—to the citadel. Beirthyr told the people they were being held as traitors, suspected of assisting Kaizyn's murder of the king. The Fae guarding the prison think they're serving their kingdom by keeping those men captive. They all believe Kaizyn murdered his own father."

"Why haven't the loyal prisoners spoken out? The guards watching them were their fellow palace guards, right? Surely they've tried to tell them what really happened?"

Etcher leveled a gaze at me. "Sevryn cut their tongues out. I mean, personally cut them out. With his own knife. Right there in the market square."

I shuddered.

"Beirthyr called it justice," Etcher said. "He praised his new alliance with Sevryn, said it was the first step to making peace between Upper Fae and Lower Fae—a new era for all of Faeside. The beginning of the end of the war."

Anger stirred in my chest. "It's going to end the war, all right. Teionyr has been attacked before, sure, but it's always managed to keep its royal vault secure because of how the wards and magic tie directly to the royals. From what I hear, the resources in that vault are immensely powerful. If the Dark Fae take full control of Teionyr and break into that vault, all the efforts the LeyGuards have put in to protect innocent Fae over the past three decades will be undone. The Dark Fae will have conquered the rest of Faeside before anyone can stop them."

The knowing expression on Etcher's face chilled me. "And why do you think they haven't taken over Teionyr and raided that vault already? Beirthyr is incapacitated—why not just kill him and seize the city? Why try to save him, why play the big charade of Beirthyr still being in control, why frame Kaizyn at all?"

I didn't have an answer for that.

Etcher stepped closer. "Sevryn knows Kaizyn didn't really commit treason, which means Beirthyr isn't the *true* heir, so long as Kaizyn lives. That means Teionyr's Seal doesn't actually protect Beirthyr, despite the magic allowing him to sear-bind. Sevryn could've killed Beirthyr at any moment, and you're right—Teionyr's palace vault is *filled* with rare faespells and treasures that could turn the tide of the war overnight. So why didn't Sevryn force Beirthyr to open it, then kill him and bring in the Dark Fae armies? Why would Sevryn need Beirthyr *alive*?"

He studied me in a way that felt like a pop quiz.

"I... I don't know," I said. "I wondered the same thing."

"Think, boy."

I realized I already had the answer. "The Teionyr Seal—it's the key to everything. So long as the Seal is active and the true heir to the throne is alive, its magic would prevent Beirthyr from accessing the royal vault. He's not the *rightful* heir, even if he could manage to secure a sear-bind."

Etcher grinned. "*There* you go."

"But keeping Beirthyr alive still doesn't fix that. To open the vault, Sevryn needs Kaizyn, not Beirthyr."

Etcher's grin widened, his next words excitedly leading me toward whatever he knew I was moments from uncovering. "But *Kaizyn* will never help him. I've spent time with him—he's honorable. And talented. He knows how to resist Selkblood sway."

"Then Sevryn needs Kaizyn dead, so that Beirthyr *will* be the rightful heir." That explained the curse.

Etcher nodded. "Yes. But Kaizyn is the sealed heir. Veilar completed that ceremony on Kaizyn years ago. So to kill him, Sevryn needs to break the Teionyr Seal, somehow."

It finally clicked together. "Sevryn's trying to find a way *around* the Seal. He knows he can't just kill Kaizyn. That explains why he's stalling here with Beirthyr. And why he came after Maddox's family Earthside, why he set up base in our town." He'd targeted Ayla and her family because of their connections to Kaizyn—both in the past, and now.

That seemed to surprise Etcher. "He went after Maddox *himself*? That explains why he was gone for several weeks, I suppose... but he must be getting desperate."

I nodded. "He is. He took big risks, and things got messy. He was reckless."

Etcher stared off in thought. "He's looking for the true name."

I froze. "The true name?"

He nodded. "Yes. The prince's true name can break the Seal, and Maddox knows the name. That knowledge was supposed to be a secret only Maddox and the Teionyrian royals knew about—but I was there. I knew he had it." He sighed. "If he's gone after Maddox, then Sevryn must know that, too. He was trying to get the name from Maddox, or find out where Maddox had recorded it."

I suddenly remembered the riddle Ayla had found. *What the prince lacks... one word carries power...* and something about flowers. Was that riddle about the true name? It could've been. Was it a clue about where to find it?

I kept quiet about the riddle in front of Etcher, though. A clue about where to find the name that could break the Seal was information way too sensitive to share with a guy who'd been lying to me for at least half the time I'd known him.

"Searching Beirthyr's mind for traces of the true name may even be part of Sevryn's reason for keeping Beirthyr alive," Etcher continued, "if you're right about Beirthyr being innocent. Either way, we have to stop Sevryn before he finds that name. If I can craft a rune that will take out enough of the guards, we could make it to the citadel and get the others to help us."

I stared at him. "You can do that? Craft a rune that could take them all out at once?" That would take an immense amount of power—and would result in a rune more potent than I might be capable of wielding.

Etcher laughed. "*Can I do it,* he asks. Who do you think you're talking to, boy? They didn't call me *Etcher* for nothing." His gaze was firm and confident as it met mine. "I can do it."

I opened my mouth, but Etcher cut me off, as though he'd read my mind.

"And you can wield it. You're strong enough, believe me. I can sense your power."

I could only hope he was right.

He waved his hand, still swinging the pen. "It'll take some planning and legwork, but I've got contacts in the city. If we can convince Sevryn to take us into the market square for supplies, I can make it happen. We've got three days, boy. If we move quickly, we can pull it off. We'll just have to hope Sevryn doesn't find the true name before then."

The blood drained from my face as my brain caught up to the missing piece of this complicated puzzle. "The true name isn't the only way to kill Kaizyn, though. Not anymore."

Etcher stopped and turned to look at me. "What do you mean?"

Panic mounted as I realized just *how* in danger Ayla might really be. "Kaizyn met her in the café—the faespell. They're bound."

"Kaizyn is *bound*? To *whom*?" Etcher stepped toward me. "Line up your words, boy. You're not making sense."

I met his eyes. "Sevryn needs *Ayla*. Maddox's granddaughter. Kaizyn came for help and in saving his life, Ayla accidentally activated a bonding faespell."

Etcher stared at me. "That's quite an accident."

My fear mounted. "I know, but listen! Kaizyn is protected by the Seal, but Ayla isn't. If he gets to her…" I sucked in a breath, trying to quell the storm of panic in my chest. "I thought getting to her was his backup plan, but it might be his *primary* plan. He brought me here as her bait. Maybe Madison, too."

Etcher's eyes widened. "Will she come for you?"

"Maybe. Probably, if she can figure out how." I stifled a curse. Desperation flooded me, and I stepped toward him. "Please. I can't let her die because of me." My heart was as tightly bound to Ayla as she was bound to Kaizyn. If she died, it would destroy me. My heart was splintering just at the thought.

But there was also more at stake than my heart. Way more. If Kaizyn died, it would destroy this whole kingdom, and all the LeyGuard *and* Upper Fae efforts to turn the tide of this war over the last two decades.

I clenched my jaw. "If either Kaizyn or Ayla dies, they *both* do. We can't let that happen."

"Then we'd better get you out of here." Etcher spun back to the table, opened the well of opalescent Runing ink, and dipped his pen in it. "Let's get to work."

I started to ask why he wasn't beginning with practice ink, but then he stepped around toward the bed where I'd placed Madison.

"But first, we should probably wake up your friend." He grabbed Madison's arm and swiped a hasty mishmash of lines on her forearm, before I could stop him.

I jumped forward and grabbed his hand. "Wait, you can't just—you're not even being careful!"

But the rune was already there, hastily painted, drying on her skin. It was no rune I'd seen before.

Etcher held up his hands. "Careful, maybe not, but effective. Just wait."

I glared at him. "What did you rune her with? I swear, if you—"

Madison woke up screaming.

# CHAPTER 15

# SILVER LIKE LIGHTNING

*Ayla*

I squinted against the bright sun, nearly blinding in contrast to the darkness of the Void. As my eyes adapted, grass and wheat fields spread out before me, with a quaint cottage to one side and the village I'd spied earlier visible in the distance.

Callan and Striker stood nearby, also squinting as their eyes adjusted.

Rory still sagged limply in Striker's arms, shockingly pale in the warm sunlight.

I glanced back at the door, but it had already snapped shut.

My heart twisted for Kaizyn.

Callan glanced over at me, then stepped closer. "As soon as we've settled Rory in and made sure he's safe, we'll go back for Kaizyn. Don't worry. He'll be fine."

I nodded, trying to feel as confident as he seemed. The thought of Kaizyn alone in the Void saddened me, but the thought of leaving Rory alone here in a strange Fae village didn't sit right with me, either. I felt caught between the two, and I hated choosing which friend to be there for. I wished I could be in both places at once.

'Dame Keyja—as Kaizyn had called her—stepped toward me. "Welcome, Ayla of the LeyGuard. I have heard much about you."

"I'm not—" I turned toward her to explain that I didn't consider myself LeyGuard, but the second part of her statement caught up to me. "You *have*?"

She smiled kindly, then spun toward Rory without further explanation. "Lower him to the ground. Let me see him."

To my surprise, Striker obeyed without question—whether because he acknowledged Keyja's authority or because he knew Rory needed the help, I wasn't sure. Maybe both.

Keyja knelt beside Rory where Striker placed him, then held her hands out and closed her eyes. Apparently, her version of *seeing* him wasn't what people usually meant by that phrase.

Her hands hovered all along his body, then her eyes popped open. Her irises flashed silver like lightning, then returned to their dark shade an instant later. She stood. "I can save him, but we'll need to work quickly." She rushed toward the cottage.

Striker scooped up Rory, and we all followed Keyja inside.

The tiny cottage's interior was cluttered but tidy. There was a small living area with a couch and table in the center, a simple kitchen area to the right with a large window, a bed against the wall to the left, and a dining table sitting in the far right corner with a lantern hanging over it. Shelves lined every open wall space, packed with books and shimmering vials in every color imaginable.

Keyja rushed from shelf to shelf, pulling out vials and books and piling them on the table.

Callan hurried toward her. "How can I help?"

Keyja gestured to the vials she'd dumped on the table without looking at Callan, her attention on the shelves. "Sort them—first by type, then by color. Are you capable?"

If Callan bristled at her doubt in him, he didn't show it. "Of course." He got right to work. There were no labels, and many of the liquids were nearly the same shades of shimmering color, but Callan quickly separated the vials into rows based on a categorization system I couldn't make sense of, as though he'd done it a million times.

My gaze drifted back to Keyja, who was now grabbing handfuls of what seemed to be herbs out of large glass jars on a shelf near the kitchen.

I tried not to gape at her large eyes, her strange clothes, her dark wings, her dusky skin, and the sparks of silvery magic that occasionally crackled from her chest. Who *was* this Fae woman? She was unlike any Fae creature *I'd* ever read about... but I wasn't really an expert in Fae species. Before all this, I hadn't even believed they existed.

Striker set Rory on the bed, then moved toward me. He leaned down close to my ear, keeping his voice low. "From the look of you, you've never seen an ArcFae." He straightened to his full height, which nearly reached the thatched ceiling, and peered down at me.

I looked up at him. "Before a couple of weeks ago, I'd never seen a *lot* of things."

Striker laughed, then his face turned serious. "You're doing well, kid. You've been through a lot these past two weeks." The compassion in his voice brought a tightness to my throat.

The worries bobbed up from where I desperately tried to keep them submerged, but they were never far beneath the surface: I'd reunited with Striker and Callan and Rory... and I'd found Kaizyn. But now we'd left Kaizyn again, Rory was in bad shape, my parents were stuck in Selkblood comas, and Reina and Madison and Champ were all still missing. And Jordan. My heart clenched. *Jordan.* We didn't even know if he was still alive.

Keyja set one last handful of herbs on the table, then swept her gaze over Callan's rows. "Well done. Thank you. Grab the bind-spells and come with me." She hurried to Rory's bedside.

Callan lifted the end of his shirt like a pouch, scooped several vials of glistening blue liquid into it, and followed her.

"Put them there." Keyja pointed to the bed, and Callan dumped the vials next to Rory. "Now back away, please."

I was still blinking at the abruptness of her instructions—and how Callan followed them without hesitation, not even a bit of his usual cheekiness—when Keyja turned toward Striker and me. "Actually, it will be best if all three of you stand back. Near the door."

We obeyed, but as she leaned over Rory, I tensed. "Why do we need to stand back?" I asked her. "What are you going to do?"

Keyja yanked the stopper from a vial and dumped a puddle of blue liquid onto Rory's chest. It was still soaking into his shirt when she glanced at me over her shoulder. "I'm going to save your friend's life."

And then lightning erupted from her chest.

# CHAPTER 16

# IT'S YOUR KING'S FUNERAL

**_Jordan_**

Madison's scream cut off, but she heaved breaths like she'd run a marathon although she was still lying flat. Her face was ghost-white, and her eyes popped open and darted wildly around the room.

I dropped to my knees beside the bed, near her face. "Are you okay?"

"*Hurts,*" she gasped, and stiffened. She arched her back and sucked quick breaths, as though preparing for another scream.

I glared at Etcher. "What did you *do* to her?!"

Etcher shrugged. "It's not me, it's the wound. I flushed the last of the venom from the bite and forced it through her system."

I jumped to my feet. "You *what*?"

"Don't worry. Sevryn gave her a faespell, right? That neutralized the toxin, but the acid in the Shadowhound bite still burns like a bugger when it moves through the body. Shadowhound venom contains a strong sedative; she would've stayed unconscious until it worked itself out of her system. We don't have time to wait for that, so I sped up the process. The pain will subside in a minute."

I glanced at Madison and decided not to punch Etcher in the face—it seemed he was right; her pain was subsiding. Her breaths were evening out, the color returning to her face.

Madison groaned again, then reached a shaky hand out for me.

I took it and squeezed her fingers briefly before letting go, just to reassure her I was there.

A guard burst through the door. "What's happening in here?"

I spun toward the door, but Etcher stepped in front of the guard. "Nothing. The girl just woke up. She's scared—and we need to go to the market for supplies!" He swept a wrinkled hand out wide, gesturing at the table. "How am I supposed to work with what's here?"

The guard peered around Etcher at Madison, scowled at me, then turned the same scowl on Etcher. "Lord Sevryn won't allow that."

Etcher crossed his bony arms. "Why don't you stop speaking *for* him like you know what he will or won't do, and tell him I need to talk to him!"

The guard grumbled, but went out and shut the door.

I glanced at the old man. "You didn't tell me we needed more supplies."

He grinned at me. "I'm working on our plan."

"What plan?" Madison asked.

I turned toward her just as Etcher answered, "The plan to get you both out of here."

I helped Madison sit up.

She leaned her head into one hand, like she had a headache. "Well, that seems like a plan I'd support."

From across the room, Etcher muttered, "But first, I need to get in touch with some contacts in the city."

I scoffed. "That's going to be a challenge. I doubt they'll let you out of here to talk to anyone, and it's not like you can send an email."

"A what?"

"Nevermind." I turned to Madison. "Are you okay?"

She glanced at me, then peered at Etcher. "I guess. Where are we? Who is *this*?"

"We're in a guarded room in the Teionyrian palace. This is Etcher. It's a long story, but he's LeyGuard—"

"Like you?"

"Yes…" I was surprised by that question—and by how easily she was accepting my answers. "Like me."

She nodded.

I studied her face. "How much do you know about any of this?"

She shrugged. "Some. Ayla and Callan explained a lot to me, at the hospital."

*Right.* She'd seen a Selkblood attack firsthand. I grimaced. "Madison, about what happened with Sevryn—I'm so sorry. If we'd known sooner that he was coming after you…"

"What happened?" Etcher asked.

Madison's voice was calmer than I expected when she answered. "He mind-controlled my father, pretended to date me, then attacked me and killed my bodyguard."

Etcher stared at her. "Sevryn? Of course he did. Why wouldn't he? Just another day in the life of a murderous Selkblood traitor."

"You think it was Sevryn *himself*?" I asked Madison.

She shivered. "Callan thought it might have been." She took a shaky breath and glanced around, then looked back at me. "You got us out of the dungeon?"

"Sort of. We're still prisoners. But I made a deal to get us moved, yes."

Her shoulders tensed. "What kind of deal?"

"The one where we help save the dying king—but only so we can figure out whether he's working with Sevryn or being manipulated and then take one or both of them down."

Madison paled. "Sevryn's here?"

I swallowed. "Yes."

Her eyes shot wide. She grabbed my arm. "I can't see him again. Please, don't make me see him again." Her fingernails dug into my skin as she clenched my arm tight.

Etcher moved in close, concerned.

I pried my arm gently from Madison's grasp, then sank to the bed next to her and put one arm around her shoulders. "It's okay, Madison. I can't guarantee you won't have to see him again, but I promise, I *will not* let him hurt you. Okay? I'll die first, before I let him hurt any more of my friends."

Madison buried her face into my shoulder. I couldn't tell if she was crying, but she clutched my shirt like it was her lifeline. Compared to the minimal interaction we usually had at school, this level of contact with her was shocking, but I supposed right now I was something familiar in a whole world of crazy.

Etcher observed us, then nodded suddenly. "That settles it."

I looked up at him. "Settles what?"

"My plan." Etcher straightened as tall as his creaky spine would allow.

For a moment, I could picture him in his true, stronger and slightly younger form, rather than as this hunched old man.

Either way, his expression brooked no argument. "When Sevryn knocks, let me do the talking. Don't say a word unless you have to, and follow my lead. Got it?"

Madison pulled back and stared at him, her eyes huge and scared. "He's coming *now*?" she squeaked.

Etcher eyed me. "Tell me something. You had a chance to use your magic in the dungeons, right? Briefly?"

I answered warily, not wanting to reveal the coin I'd used. "Yes."

"Was it like your usual magic? Did it feel different, in any way?"

I thought back. "Actually, it *was* a little wonky. My flame was hard to wield, at first, and then when I activated the special rune, it was way more powerful than I expected. But I thought it was just the rune. Why?"

Etcher skirted my gaze. "No reason!"

Now I was *definitely* suspicious. I started to question him, but then we heard Sevryn's sharp command out in the hall. "Unlock the door!"

Madison jumped up from the bed and scurried behind me, clutching the back of my shirt.

Etcher stepped in front of us both, then glanced back at Madison over his shoulder. "Don't worry, sweetheart; we've got you. He won't touch a single hair."

I stared at him with a sudden burst of gratitude.

The doorknob jiggled as the guard worked the key, then turned.

Etcher grinned. "Showtime."

Sevryn strode into the room, already in a mood.

"That's him," Madison whimpered behind me, digging her grip more deeply into my shirt.

Sevryn pinned Etcher with a deadly glare. "What's the problem? I already provided you with all the standard materials for Runing."

Etcher waved his hands dismissively. "Yes, yes, but this isn't a *standard* sort of rune, is it? I need specialized supplies! Who's the expert here? Do you *want* our patient to combust or implode?" He cut his glance to the guard, who still lingered at the door, then leaned close to Sevryn and lowered his voice to a whisper. "Because I'm telling you, without the proper materials, that's a likely outcome."

To my surprise, Sevryn didn't attack us on the spot—though he did cast a chilling glance at Madison that set me instantly on edge.

Instead, Sevryn clenched his jaw, pulled back and crossed his arms, then huffed in annoyance and asked through gritted teeth: "And where would one *get* these supplies?"

Etcher straightened with a grin. "I know just the place! An old apothecarist in the market square. He used to be a *royal* apothecarist until *you Dark Fae* drove him out."

A glare from Sevryn cut Etcher's tangent short.

"Anyway," Etcher shrugged, "he'll have what I need."

Sevryn stared daggers at Etcher for a few long moments, then sighed. "Fine. Write me a list and I'll see that it's done."

Etcher balked. "You only gave me three days to make this rune—and now I'll have to wait a whole day while your men bumble around the city, trying to track down my supplies? And probably the *wrong* ones based on what they brought me this first time. Do I get an extension for their incompetence?"

Sevryn's jaw ticked again. "No," he growled. "Just work faster."

Etcher rolled his eyes. "Rushed work makes shoddy work, but hey, it's your king's funeral."

Sevryn glared at him. "*Fine*. I'll purchase the supplies personally, to make sure it's done right—but I'm no fool. I'm not leaving you here without my supervision. You're going *with* me, under full guard. You will give me a map *ahead of time* of where we're going, you will make an *exact list* of what you need, and when we're there you will pick out the supplies *yourself*, so you can't claim they aren't the right ones. And if you try *anything* while we're out in the city, I'll kill you on the spot and find myself another Runist. Understand?"

Etcher glanced back and wiggled his eyebrows at me.

I tensed. Was he *trying* to get us killed?

Sevryn saw it, too, and turned his glare on me. "I don't know what you're up to, LeyGuard brat, but I'm not about to leave you unguarded in the palace while I'm gone. You're *all* coming. All three of you"—he shot a pointed glance at Madison—"and you'll all be fully cuffed and guarded. Any tricks and I'll kill you *all*." He glared at each of us.

Madison's arm trembled against my back where she still clenched my shirt.

Sevryn stepped back. "Make your list, draw your map, and do whatever else you need to do to get ready. We leave in twenty minutes."

He stormed out and slammed the door. The deadbolt thunked shut from outside.

I turned to Etcher. "What just happened?"

Etcher grinned. "I got us a trip into the city."

# Chapter 17

# Sentient Ball of Lightning

*Ayla*

I watched in disbelief as the lightning bolt from Keyja's chest took shape beside her into an enormous, glowing creature that quickly faded into a very solid, very *real* animal with huge, dark eyes and thick brown fur. It resembled a massive bison, with its head reaching nearly to the cottage ceiling. Well, if bison usually had crackles of electricity snapping out into the air from their skin—which this thing did.

Keyja rattled off something that seemed like instructions to the electro-bison in another language, then grabbed a thick quilt from a shelf near the bed and spread it over Rory's faespell-soaked chest.

My nerves jumped as the bison creature lowered its immense face toward Rory. I stepped toward Keyja. "What is *that*? What is it doing?"

Keyja glanced over her shoulder at me, but her eyes had gone lightning-white, like two glowing orbs.

I gasped in shock, but Callan grabbed my arm and pulled me back.

"Easy, Ayla. Let them work."

Panic pinged through my chest, but I bit my tongue and held still. I trusted Callan. I knew he wouldn't let anything harm Rory. And apparently, Callan trusted Keyja.

Keyja turned her face back toward the bison, raised her hands over Rory's face, and said something else in the words I couldn't understand.

The animal nodded, then it gently pressed its nose to the blanket over Rory's chest.

Its face was so massive it covered Rory's entire torso. Waves of glowing energy flowed out from where it touched him, spreading across his chest and wrapping around his sides, making a circuit around him. Every few seconds, fresh sparks crackled out from the creature's nose to join the moving glow.

"What is... Is it hurting him?" But even as I asked, I could see it wasn't. Rory's face had taken on a calm look, like he was in a peaceful dream. I eyed the bison, still uncomfortable with its unknown magic channeling into my friend.

"What *is* that thing?" I whispered to Callan.

Callan leaned near me. "That *thing* is Tofa—the last remaining striniak of Arcvale."

My mind flooded with questions as I glanced at him, but he continued in a low voice.

"She's *incredibly* powerful. Her magic feeds the dome that protects Arcvale, and is said to be the source of the ArcFae's power, the energy that powers each individual's archeart. She's sacred to the ArcFae. Only the bonded one can touch her directly; anyone else will die instantly."

Well, that explained the blanket. But this sacred bison had come out of Keyja's *chest*.

Callan seemed to anticipate my question as I stared back at him. "Keyja was bonded to Tofa's mother, the previous striniak. There is only ever one striniak at a time. When the next is born, the mother passes her power to the youngling, then the mother's spirit moves on to the beyond. But each striniak must choose an ArcFae to be its bonded one, an ArcFae who is gifted the ability to touch the striniak directly so that they can assist—when the time comes—in the next striniak's birth. Dahlia, Tofa's mother, chose Keyja herself as an infant, as her bonded one. No one understood why—Keyja was an outcast to her people, considered unfit.

She was the only female ArcFae ever known to have been born without an archeart. The elders nearly killed her at birth for the defect."

A small gasp escaped me. "They would do that?"

Callan nodded. "Even once chosen, she was still never fully accepted by most of her people," he answered softly. "They believed the striniak's choice had been a mistake, that Keyja was not strong enough to fulfill her sacred duty. That she would doom her people."

I looked at Keyja, trying to wrap my mind around that, around what her childhood must have been like.

Callan nodded toward the bed, where Tofa's snout had lit up like a stream of energy, spreading a glow through the blanket over Rory's chest. "It was fate; a pairing meant to be. The darklings chose the time of Dahlia's labor to attack, when the dome was unstable. Keyja had just come of age and she helped Dahlia birth Tofa herself while chaos descended around them. When Tofa was at her most vulnerable, Keyja risked her life to save her—and in return, Tofa *became* Keyja's archeart." He shrugged. "At least, in a sense. They need each other."

"So... ArcFae don't *usually* house glowing, magical bisons in their chests?" I whispered back.

Striker laughed from beside me. "No. Not usually. It's like housing a sentient ball of lightning—it's *never* happened before, that we know."

Callan nodded his agreement. "But Keyja and Tofa work best *together*, like a team. Two halves of a whole."

"Oh." I could understand, now, why people treated Keyja with such deference. Still, the sight of a crackling bison-snout pressed to Rory's chest was unnerving. "And their power is... healing him?"

Keyja pulled her hands back from Rory's face and looked at me. "Not healing. Healed." She said something to Tofa in the foreign words.

Tofa stepped back, lifting her face away from Rory. The glow faded from the bison-creature's snout. Her massive head flicked toward me, and her enormous, dark eyes locked on me for a moment. Tofa nodded at me—a single, slow nod—then she flared into a blinding, crackling light that snapped in on itself and vanished back into the hole in Keyja's chest.

I stared at the crackling orb on Keyja's chest for a long moment before I came to myself and realized how rude my stare probably was—Keyja was now staring at *me*.

"I'm sorry, I just—I've never seen anything like that before." My face flushed hot.

Keyja laughed softly. "I understand. Not many have." She smiled kindly. "Tofa likes you. She sees courage in you. And honor. A willingness to risk self in protection of friends."

I smiled weakly back at her, suddenly feeling tears press behind my eyes. "Thank you. I'm trying." I stepped toward her, eager to check on Rory. "Will he be okay?"

Keyja nodded. "He will be." She waved me closer as she leaned over and slid the blanket from his chest. "The binding liquid will stop any venom or dark magic from spreading further, and Tofa's healing will do the rest. Now, your friend needs only sleep and time."

The pool of faespell liquid had soaked in to Rory's skin, but there was still a purplish wet spot on his shirt from it. "You said venom? And dark magic?"

"Yes," Keyja said, as though it should be obvious. "The creature that attacked him was of dark magic. I could see that in the wound, even without seeing the beast itself. Darkness like that spreads, if left unchecked. It would have killed him within hours." She smiled at me. "Do not worry, though. The darkness has been seared away, now. He will recover just fine."

I stared at Rory's pale face, and the realization of what *could* have happened to him washed over me. I felt suddenly lightheaded.

Keyja reached out to steady me as I swayed. "You need rest." Her voice was commanding, but her hands were gentle as she pushed me toward the bed. "Sit."

I sank onto the mattress beside Rory's legs.

In an instant, Callan was at my side with an armful of extra blankets he'd grabbed from somewhere.

"Put them there on the floor," Keyja told him.

As he spread out a pallet beside Rory's bed, Keyja's dark eyes locked on mine. "I will make you food. You will eat, and then you will sleep."

Her tone made it clear that she would accept no argument, but I wasn't inclined to argue, anyway—I was *exhausted,* the weight of the past day I'd spent in the Veil settling in on me. "Yes," I said weakly. Spots were forming in my vision. "Okay."

Keyja bustled over to the kitchen area, and a few moments later, Striker's massive hands shoved a metal cup of water and a plate of sandwich at me. "It's kind of like a veggie burger," Striker said. "But don't worry; it's edible."

The bread had a dense, oaty look, like the homemade bread my mom had attempted during Thanksgiving one year, and the fillings were mostly vegetable-looking—lettuce and something like a tomato though it was green—with a crispy-looking patty of a meatish substance that smelled spicy, like pepper.

"Eat, kid," Striker said. "You'll feel better once you do."

I didn't feel that hungry—I really just wanted to sleep—but I knew he was right. I forced down as many bites of the mystery sandwich as I could and found it was actually pretty good.

Callan and Striker hovered around the table near the kitchen, eating sandwiches of their own.

I got about half of the sandwich and most of the water down before my stomach protested it was full.

Keyja took the plate and cup from me. "Sleep," she said again, and I obediently nestled down into the pallet Callan had made for me.

"Striker? Callan?" Sleep's claws were already pulling at me, my eyes drifting closed. "What about you?"

"We'll sleep too, kid," Striker answered. "But don't worry. One of us will watch over you. You're safe."

I meant to respond, but I was already slipping into slumber.

# Chapter 18

# SOS

*Ayla*

I woke to the sound of Rory's voice. "Ayla?"

I pushed up from my blankets on the floor and found him staring down at me from the bed.

He sat up, winced, then leaned back against his pillow. "Where are we?" His skin had its color back, which brought me a sigh of relief.

"Um…" I shifted so I could lean back against the bed and looked around. We were alone in the cottage, for the moment. I had no idea how to explain Keyja or the striniak, so I went for the most important info. "We're with friends. We're safe."

Rory glanced down at his faespell-stained shirt, then lifted it and gently fingered the cloth wrap Kaizyn had placed beneath. "I remember being in the dark… and something attacked me. I thought I—" He shuddered. "How did I get here?"

"Callan protected you, then Striker found the both of you, and they brought you to Prince Kaizyn and me at his hideout. Kaizyn did what he could for you but it wasn't enough, so we brought you here for help. The woman who lives here is a healer, of sorts."

Rory's eyes widened. "You found the Fae prince?" He glanced around the cottage again. "Is Madison here, too?"

My heart sank. "No, I'm sorry. We still haven't found her."

Rory's face paled again. "*What*? We have to go look for her!" He threw back the covers and swung his legs over the side of the bed to stand, but he barely made it two inches off the bed before he swayed and plopped back onto the mattress, clutching his shoulder. "Wow, I'm dizzy."

"Easy!" I stood and reached over to hold him in place. "You're still healing. Rory—you nearly *died*. You have to rest."

His eyes were glassy, but when they cleared, he narrowed them on me. "We can't just sit around while she's missing!"

I sighed. "I know, Rory. And trust me... Callan knows, too. He's as committed to bringing Madison back safely as you are. But we've only been in the Veil about a day, and we don't know where she is, yet." I gripped his hand and locked my eyes on his. "We're not giving up. We will find her. As soon as Keyja gets back, I'll ask her to help us. She might know something."

Rory sucked a shallow breath, then nodded. "Okay." He glanced around. "I take it Keyja is this healer you mentioned?"

I nodded. "Yes. But she's—"

I didn't get to finish preparing Rory for what to expect, because the cottage door swung open and Keyja, Callan, and Striker all walked in. Keyja held an armful of what looked like wheat stalks.

"Hey, kid!" Striker smiled at me. "Good to see you awake." He turned his smile on Rory. "And you, too. You gave us all a scare." He offered Rory his hand. "I'm Striker, one of the LeyGuard." He gestured behind him. "You already know Callan. And this is 'Dame Keyja, the one who healed you."

Rory's eyes swept over Striker's massive form and Keyja's sparking chest and long wings, but to his credit, only a flicker of shock showed in his expression, and it vanished almost instantly.

He returned Striker's handshake. "Nice to meet you both." He swept his gaze over the three of them. "Thank you, all of you, for saving my life."

Keyja nodded a silent acceptance of his thanks, then walked over to set her armful of wheat on the table.

"You're welcome, kid," Striker said, then dropped his pack and a knife he was holding onto the table next to Keyja's wheat and my pack from earlier, which as far as I remembered, I'd still been wearing when I fell asleep. They must've slipped it off me to make me more comfortable.

Striker and Callan both looked calm, so I gathered their outing had just been a walk, or maybe to help Keyja gather wheat.

Callan moved toward the bed. "I'm glad you're okay—" he said, but Rory interrupted him.

"We have to find Madison."

Callan tensed. "We're working on it. Striker and I were just discussing some potential leads with 'Dame Keyja, sources that might be able to find us info on Madison, Jordan, Reina, even the dog."

I glanced between him and Keyja. "You were?"

"Yes." Keyja said. "None of my contacts have located any of your allies, yet, but Faeside is a big place, and many creatures have ears. If your friends are still Faeside, we'll find them. It's just a matter of time."

Callan nodded his agreement. "Someone has to have seen or heard something."

Rory still looked agitated, which I completely understood, but I was relieved Keyja and Callan had already put out feelers for information.

"We'll find them," Callan said again, and he seemed utterly confident.

"How can you *know*?" Rory blurted. "Is that some kind of Fae ability?" His eyes held anger, though I doubted it was Callan he was truly angry with. I knew from experience that fear could also manifest as anger.

Callan dropped his hands to his sides. "No, I just—I just know."

Rory stared at him a moment, then nodded, though he still looked tense. "I hope you're right."

"They're okay." Callan said, glancing between Rory and me. "They're *all* okay. We just have to find them."

I think we all knew Callan could be wrong, but it helped not to say it. There was something reassuring about his certainty.

I felt myself nodding, too. "Yeah. Okay." I *wanted* to believe him, but somewhere deep inside me lurked the anxious voice that, as always, kept trying to prepare me for the worst. Still, his confidence helped a little.

"Keep belief," Keyja said kindly. "It will just take time to locate them. You are welcome to remain here, while you wait."

"Thank you," I said, then drew a breath, thinking of Keyja's many faespells. "My parents are in a Selkblood coma back at the Hub. Can you and Tofa... I mean, is there something you can do? A faespell? Anything?"

A thread of hope spread through me. If she could heal Rory, then surely—

Keyja shook her head. "I'm afraid not. I'm sorry." Her regret seemed sincere. "That's beyond my ability."

My hope sank.

"What about Maxim Warwick?" Callan asked. "He was an apothecarist at the palace, under King Veilar's rule. He vanished during Beirthyr's uprising, but rumors say he's still in Teionyr, hiding out somewhere. He was incredibly talented with faespells—might such a thing be within his capabilities?"

"I have not heard of him," Keyja said, "but if he is highly skilled, he may be capable. Faespells were always more of my mother's gift than mine, but a powerful apothecarist might be able to make a counterspell to the Selkblood trance, yes. I believe my mother could have concocted such a faespell when she was here. Arcvale and its dome helped fuel her power. Now, in her current state... I am not so sure."

I opened my mouth to ask more about Keyja's mother, but a high-pitched alarm from Striker's waist arrested my attention.

Striker snatched a palm-sized, disc-like device from his belt. A light on it was flashing red.

Striker cursed under his breath. "SOS. From Brone at the Hub."

"*What?*" Panic shot through me.

Striker looked up at me, and I could see the battle in his eyes. "I'm sorry, Ayla. The safest place for you right now is here, for both your and Kaizyn's sakes, but Brone would never send this unless—"

"Go," I interrupted him. "*Please*. Make sure my family is okay."

Callan stepped toward me. "I'll make sure Ayla stays safe," he told Striker.

Striker glanced between Callan and me, then nodded. "All right." He turned to Keyja. "What's the fastest way to a LeyGate?"

"There's an inactive one on the northwest side of the dome. It's sealed from this side, but your magic should open it. It leads to our nearest Earthside refuge, just outside Hub boundaries."

"Thank you." He grabbed the knife he had left on the table with our packs and slid it into his belt. "The LeyGuard owes you for all your help."

"The LeyGuard helped me save a remnant of my people," she said. "You owe me nothing."

Striker nodded, then turned to me. "Be smart, kid. Stay safe. I'll be back as soon as I can."

He rushed outside.

My insides felt like a mass of tangled worry-ropes, all knotted together with concerns for my loved ones.

Callan stepped toward me, his movements quick and purposeful—like he was back in battle mode. "I need to go check on Kaizyn. You and Rory will be safe here, with Keyj—"

"No." I clenched my fists. I couldn't take just sitting around, worrying. I needed to move. "I'm going with you."

Callan's face softened. "Ayla, I don't think that's a good—"

*Ayla.* A thunderous voice cut into my mind. *Ayla Rogers.*

I stiffened, and Callan's eyes widened. "What is it?"

The voice continued. *Ayla—come outside.*

I stared up at Callan. "It's a voice in my head."

"Like, talking to you through your mind-gift?" he asked.

"I don't know. Maybe?"

"What did it say?"

"Just my name, and to come outside."

Callan and Rory both stared at me—Rory with curiosity, Callan with concern.

"You can hear voices in your *mind*?" Rory asked.

Keyja stepped around in front of me. "Do you recognize the voice?"

I shook my head. "No. Definitely not. It's like thunder, almost. I've never heard anything like it."

"Isn't your mind-gift only supposed to work if you know the person already?" Callan asked. "I thought it had to be someone you were familiar with."

I nodded. "Usually, yes, but this—"

"It's the Eldervine," Keyja said.

I turned to her. "*What*?"

"The Eldervine. His kind possesses a talent for mindspeak. If you have your grandfather's mind-gift, he could easily speak to you through it. I had wondered if he would attempt to contact you."

"The *Eldervine*?" Callan seemed shocked, but not alarmed, which I took as a good sign.

"Why would he want to contact *me*?" I asked.

"What's an Eldervine?" Rory asked over the top of my question—which had been the next question I planned to ask.

Keyja glanced at him, then turned back to me. "I think it will be better if I show you, and then you can ask him yourself."

She walked toward her front door, and I hurried to follow.

"Wait! I'm coming, too," Rory said. He winced as he sat up, and Callan helped him to his feet. Rory moved slowly, but he seemed steady enough as he walked toward the door, which gave my heart some peace.

What did *not* give me peace was what I saw when Keyja swung her front door open.

There, standing in the grass in front of her cottage, was a massive plant that *definitely* had not been there before. It was the size of a redwood, but just an enormous, green stalk. I had to crane my neck back to see the burst of thin branches with shoots of leaves on top of it, almost like a shock of hair. If it wasn't so massive, I would've thought it was a giant stalk of celery.

*Hello, Ayla Rogers,* the voice rumbled in my mind again, though the plant had no face or any visible way of speaking. *I am Mraugathal, the last Eldervine of Upper Faeside.* The leaves atop its massive body quivered. *I have waited a long time to meet you.*

# CHAPTER 19

# A Very Special Sort of Ink

**_Jordan_**

Sevryn led us, under a contingent of six Fae guards armed with an array of weapons, through the palace corridors and out into a common area of the palace—a large indoor courtyard with a fountain and vaulted ceilings.

The inner supports of the ceiling were carved with elaborate sculptures of various animals, and inset with stained-glass displays of various nature scenes—cloud-topped mountains, sunset-lit waterfalls, forests with bright flowers—that I suspected were locations found in the areas surrounding Teionyr. It was really quite stunning, except that it echoed with the emptiness of a place that wasn't meant to be empty. The wide-open foyer area was probably once bustling with visitors and servants, but now it was occupied only by armed guards protecting the various doorways that led off the courtyard into other areas of the palace.

Madison walked nervously beside me, fiddling with the rune-cuff on her wrist.

Etcher ambled behind us, acting like he had all the time in the world—until one guard prodded him in the rear with a sword when he fell behind the rest of us, which got him moving more quickly.

Sevryn led our guarded group across the floor of the courtyard—a bright mosaic of various colors of polished stone tiles—to a large, heavy door guarded by two Fae armed with both swords and guns like the one I'd seen on the guard in the prison.

At Sevryn's nod, the guards stepped inward and pushed open the palace doors. It was daylight outside. From the sun it looked like perhaps early morning, though I knew the sun's light could play differently here in Faeside than Earthside.

As the doors spread further open, a clear view of the rest of Teionyr spread out over the slope in front of the palace. Teionyr's royal city was effectively a big, walled square, and the Teionyrian palace sat on a hilltop on one edge of that square, protected from behind by the sheer rock wall of a mountain range. Row upon row of tall housing structures, made of what looked like mud-brick, formed the rest of the city. From our vantage point, I could see straight past the rows sloping down the hill, to another square sectioned off in the center of all the housing—the market square, where we were headed.

The guards led us down the sloped street and into the alleys of the city. Sevryn kept a tight grip on Etcher's hand-drawn map and walked behind us, which surprised me at first, but he definitely did not walk with the air of someone who was *following*. He was still in charge, only from the rear—probably to make sure we couldn't escape.

We quickly reached lower ground, where I could no longer see beyond the height of the housing structures which surrounded us. Tan, mud-brick buildings loomed on every side, with glassless window openings, and brown, packed-dirt paths formed alleys off the main street, which was also packed dirt. Occasional flowering plants or colorful laundry in the windows, along with the bright green vines that grew up the walls of some buildings, were the only color in an otherwise all-brown landscape. Other than the sunny, blue sky above, of course.

I stayed close to Madison, ready to protect her if needed. I tried not to glance back at Etcher, though I was still intensely curious about his plan for our time in the city. Etcher had told me only that we needed to contact someone in the market square. He refused to say more, because the Fae could be listening. I supposed he was right to be cautious, but not knowing what to expect still had me on edge.

There weren't many Teionyrians out on the streets, but those we saw were mostly adults with tanned skin, dark hair, and dark eyes similar to Callan's. Most of them seemed strong and healthy, overall, but there was something about the way their eyes immediately averted at the sight of us that stirred an uneasy feeling in my stomach. None spoke to us, and those who let their gazes linger on us in curiosity for a few moments quickly hurried away afterward.

The streets were quiet, save a subtle murmur of commotion in the direction of the market. I wondered if there were children in Teionyr, since I hadn't seen any, but—there must be, right? They were probably all inside.

A low hum of commotion and conversation reached us as the market square came into view, intensifying as we drew closer. The market was a stark difference from the deserted streets we'd passed on the way, and clearly where the day-to-day activity in Teionyr happened. There were people *everywhere.* Colorful, open-faced tents stood all around, with vendors selling wares. Signs hung in front of each booth, declaring their specialties. In the center of the square stood a gallows. *Yikes.* Not exactly your friendly market vibe, though the people didn't seem overly bothered as they milled around it, conversing and shopping and selling.

Mud-brick walls bordered three sides of the market square, with narrow alleys between them, including the one we'd come through. Above the height of the market tents, a smattering of windows peeked out from the walls. Some windowsills held flower pots and other windows held washing hung out to dry, suggesting those three walls were actually the sides of more housing structures. The fourth wall of the marketplace was a looming, grey stone wall that felt like a dark shadow compared to the bright colors of the market tents. A metal-barred entry gate hunkered in the center of that wall, like a prison door.

Etcher leaned near me. "That's the citadel," he whispered. "Where they're keeping the other guards."

So it *was* a prison. Fittingly designed, then. Other than the few bright green vines trailing up its walls, the whole structure screamed doom and gloom—major *Abandon hope, all ye who enter* vibes.

"Let's go," Sevryn barked from behind us.

The crowds gave our procession a wide berth, especially when they saw Sevryn was part of it. People glanced away or murmured in hushed voices to one another behind their hands.

Despite that tension, I heard laughter, and I smiled when I saw there *were* children. A large circle of them played a game in a space between the tents on one side of the square, involving a stick the kids tossed back and forth while they chanted, then one kid ran across the circle—almost like a blend of Red Rover and Hot Potato. I wondered what the rules were, but I tore my attention away from the kids when I heard Sevryn talking to our guards.

"Stay alert; let no one near the prisoners." He moved up into the lead of our group.

Etcher shrugged at me, and I wondered yet again about his plan.

I glanced back at Madison. Her gaze was on the children, but when she saw me looking at her, she gave me a weak smile. I wondered if she had also thought of the P.E. games we'd played in school... but I didn't dare ask her, not with the way Sevryn kept glaring at us. If I said *anything* to Madison, Sevryn would probably think we were conspiring to escape.

Not that that would be the worst idea...

But it probably wouldn't work, so I couldn't risk it.

Sevryn stopped our group at a gap between tents, with nothing in front of us but one of the housing structures and a window high above us.

He gestured for the guards to push Etcher toward him. "This shows the supply shop *here*." He jabbed a finger at the map. "This is nothing but a blank wall."

Etcher grinned. "Knock."

Sevryn glared at him, then rapped on the mud-brick wall with his knuckles.

His knock couldn't have been heard over the market commotion, but a head poked out of the window several feet above, anyway.

An old man with a scraggly beard and two dark eyes stared down at us from the window. "I'm closed!" The man's face paled as he noticed Sevryn. "Oh. My apologies! One moment."

A moment later, a bucket swung down on a rope, nearly hitting a guard in the head.

"If Lord Beirthyr requires something, let me know what you need, then place your payment in the bucket," the man called down. "I'll make it right away, though I'm low on arrowfen, at the moment, so I—"

"*King* Beirthyr does require something," Sevryn snapped back. "Etcher, tell him your requests."

The man's eyes flicked to Etcher and widened in surprise for a moment, I thought, though if so, he covered it quickly. "Sorry to offend," he told Sevryn, then turned back to Etcher. "Do you have a list of ingredients?"

Etcher rattled off several types of special Runing ink, plus an innocuous healing faespell I recognized from my studies.

"What is that for?" Sevryn asked.

Etcher stared at him like it was a dumb question. "To stir into the ink. It imbues it with additional healing effects."

Sevryn crossed his arms. "Very well. Is that all?"

"Yes."

Sevryn stared up at the man in the window. "How quickly can you have this all ready?"

"I can have it delivered to the palace within the hour."

Sevryn glared up at him. "We'll wait. How much do we owe you?"

"Sixty-five barglans," the man called down.

Sevryn narrowed his eyes. "That's quite a lot for ink and one healing spell, isn't it?"

"It's a very special sort of ink. Rare ingredients. Only for Runing." The man's eyes caught on Etcher's.

"Yes," Etcher agreed. "The LeyGuards used to import it from Teionyr, for their specialized runes." He looked at Sevryn. "And we're asking for a rush job, which always costs extra."

Sevryn glared at Etcher and then the man. "Very well. But if I find you've misled me or tampered with *anything*, either of you, you'll be the next on that gallows. Understood?"

The man's eyes lingered on Etcher a moment, then he nodded slowly. "Yes, of course."

Sevryn placed some coins in the bucket and the man hauled it up.

Sevryn spun to Madison, Etcher, and me. "Sit there." He pointed to the wall beneath the window. "Backs against the wall."

We sat, with me in the middle and Etcher and Madison on either side, nearly touching my shoulders.

The guards flanked us while Sevryn paced impatiently.

We waited.

Time passed slowly and awkwardly, with no one speaking, but eventually the bucket lowered. A faespell and several bottles of glistening ink sat inside.

Sevryn took the goods and slid them into a satchel a guard handed him, then slipped the satchel on with its strap secured across his chest.

The man said goodnight and hauled up the empty bucket, and we left.

On the walk back through the city, Sevryn said nothing. When we reached the palace, he escorted us back to our guarded room and shoved the satchel of supplies at Etcher.

"Get to work!" he yelled, then slammed the door in our faces.

The door lock thunked closed.

Madison sank onto the bed.

I turned to Etcher, keeping my voice low. "That Fae was your contact, right? I thought you were going to pass him a message—was there a code hidden in what you asked for?"

"Didn't have to code anything," Etcher said. "Just seeing my face was enough." He fingered the vials he'd pulled from the satchel. "Maxim knows me well enough to know that if I've brought a Dark Fae to his doorstep, it's because I want him dead."

"You want your *contact* dead?" Madison asked.

Etcher stared at her. "No. The Dark Fae." He held up a vial to the light. "But more importantly..." He tilted the vial, and a sliver of something white peeked out from the glistening liquid.

Etcher hurried to the table, popped the stopper loose from the vial, then grabbed tweezers from the tools he'd spread out earlier. He extracted a tiny scroll of waxy paper from the vial. It left drips of faespell on the blank parchment on the table, but Etcher didn't seem to care. He re-stoppered the vial and set it down, carefully unrolled the tiny scroll, then looked up at me. "You're right. Your girl is Faeside."

"What?" I reached for the paper.

Small, scrunched handwriting covered it in glossy black ink. *The tiger is bound. The rope will be severed. Darkness scours the Veil.*

I looked at Etcher. "What does it mean?"

"Kaizyn is the tiger," he said. "We started calling him that as a lad, when he bonded to his fire-cat."

Kaizyn was bonded to a *fire-cat?* That was an interesting bit of info. But not the important thing right now.

"The rope would be your girl," he continued. "Seems word's gotten around among the resistance that Kaizyn's fate is bound to a human's."

"The resistance?" Madison asked, but my attention was back on the scroll.

"*The rope will be severed...* Does that mean..." My blood ran cold as the message clicked.

Etcher met my wide-eyed stare. "Her death means his death. The Dark Fae are hunting your girl in the Veil, and they intend to kill her."

"No." Instant adrenaline shot through every vein. "No! We've got to—"

The door swung open and Sevryn charged in. "A message." He snatched the paper right out of my fingers like the strike of a snake, before I could even respond. His eyes flashed with fury. "I knew I couldn't trust you."

# Chapter 20
# Everything Is Connected

**Ayla**

*I* *have waited a long time to meet you.*

Mraugathal's voice thundered in my mind as I stepped out into the grass.

Keyja and Callan both gave quick bows to the giant plant creature in front of me.

Not wanting to offend, I hurriedly followed their lead.

Beside me, I saw Rory do the same.

*I could feel your mind calling to me, Ayla Rogers,* the Eldervine continued.

"You could?" I definitely hadn't *intended* to call him.

*Yes.* The leaves at the top of the stalk quivered excitedly. *We knew your grandfather well. Since we first heard of your birth, we have awaited your visit.*

That statement was nearly as baffling as trying to figure out where on the giant plant-stalk to focus my eye contact as I raised from my clumsy bow. I glanced at Keyja again and saw that her eyes seemed focused slightly upward, just above her own eye level. I copied, praying Eldervines weren't easily offended.

"We?" I asked. *Hadn't he said he was the last Eldervine?* "Are there more like you, here?" I glanced around, but saw only the open fields.

A low rumble echoed through my head, threaded with a feeling of mirth, that I took to be a chuckle. Only then did I realize that the Eldervine's speech was more complex than the usual mind-gift hearing; I could also *feel* his words, a tinge of the emotion with which he said them.

*More Eldervines? No.* A wave of sadness washed in with his words, then receded like the tide. *But we are many. We are all connected—cousins, each with our own brothers and sisters, mothers and fathers and aunts and uncles, grandparents and grandchildren. Though for me, there are only cousins.*

Suddenly, an image appeared in my mind of a thick forest of vines, trees, shrubs, grasses, all thriving and green, and then flickers of other images—vine tendrils wrapped around the branches of larger trees; weeds and shrubs of various species growing side by side, intertwining with one another's offshoots; and all of them sharing a tangled, interconnected web of roots beneath the ground.

*We are not all the same, yet we are one.* A shade of pride seeped in with Mraugathal's words as the images faded. *Do you understand?*

"I think so, yes." I'd seen plenty of intertwined plants in wooded areas back home, and I'd even heard of some research studies that discovered massive underground communication networks among root systems and fungi, but interconnected plant societies that could speak directly into my mind were definitely something new. "Can they all mindspeak, like you?"

Again, Mraugathal chuckled. *No. Only an Eldervine can speak outside ourselves in this way—though we speak among ourselves freely. The others cannot speak to you—but they can hear.*

Well, that wasn't creepy at all...

*I am happy to meet you, Ayla. Maddox was the last human to hear my voice, and to allow me in his mind this way. We are pleased you have inherited his gift... and something more.*

"Something more?" I asked. "You mean... my other magic? You can sense that?"

Keyja glanced at me, and I realized the rest of them couldn't hear Mraugathal; they could only hear my side of the conversation.

"You have *magic*?" Rory asked in surprise, and it suddenly occurred to me what a weird day he must be having. He'd been even less prepared for all this craziness than I was.

*Your other power feels erratic,* Mraugathal said. *Powerful but clumsy, like an oriliak calfling.*

A nervous chuckle escaped me. "It feels erratic to me, too. I've only just discovered it. I'm not even sure what it can do."

"She has some kind of ice powers," I heard Callan whisper to Rory, "though we aren't sure yet how they work, or what triggered them. It's not a normal ability for LeyGuards."

*It* is *LeyGuard magic,* Mraugathal said, and I could feel the curiosity in his voice, *but also not. It is... tangled with Fae energy, somehow. I see the bond between you and the prince—but this is something more. Both LeyGuard and not.*

A small gasp escaped me. "You can *see* that?"

*Yes,* Mraugathal answered. *And many other things.*

I tried not to veer off into wondering what *that* meant.

"Eldervines can sense magic," Keyja chimed in softly, "the same way *all* plants can sense light and energy. Magic and light and energy are all connected, for them."

*Everything is connected, for us,* the Eldervine said.

The thought felt distant, as though directed at someone else. Was he responding to Keyja but allowing me also to hear?

I turned to her. "Can you hear him, too?"

She nodded. "When he wishes me to."

"*I* can't hear anything," Rory mumbled.

Keyja chuckled. "Not all humans can hear Eldervines, but ArcFae are attuned to their energy; we cannot mindspeak *to* them, but we can receive." She turned back to me. "Whatever this new magic is, perhaps Mraugathal can help you identify it."

I stared up at Mraugathal. "Would you? I mean—if you can?"

His response rode into my mind on a wave of energy that felt like a smile. *I will try. But first—the reason I came.* The smile darkened and shifted into a sense of urgency. *Are there others of your kind here? Those who came with you through the Veil?*

My heart leaped. "Yes! There were others—my friends. Jordan, Reina, and Madison... and Jordan's dog, Champ. Jordan and Madison were taken here by Fae, and the others were sucked through by something. We got separated." Hope sparked in my chest. "Have you seen them?"

The leaves rustled again. *Picture them, child. Let me be sure.*

Jordan's face was first to spring to my mind. My heart squeezed as his golden eyes came into view, his gaze as intense in my mind as it had been the last time I saw him—right after we'd kissed. It *hurt* to picture him like this, not knowing when I might see him again. But I also didn't want to let the image go. For now, it was all I had.

A warm buzz of sympathy swept through my mind. *Good, child. Good. Keep going.*

Reluctantly, I pushed the image of Jordan away and focused on my other friends. Reina, with her fiery hair and green eyes and bubbly smile—at least, it had been bubbly before all this; before Jordan had been taken. Pain tinged my image of her, too, but Mraugathal's voice held me steady.

*Keep going.*

I pictured Madison—her blonde hair perfectly styled as always, and then another, the more disheveled version, like she'd looked in the hospital. The wave of affection I felt at the thought of her surprised me. I really had come to think of her as a friend.

Rory stepped close. "What's he saying, Ayla? Has he seen them? Has he seen Madison?"

I waved a hand to shush him as I pushed the last image through—one of Champ. His white fur, his goofy dog-grin with his tongue lolling out, his whole body wagging like it did when he saw Jordan or Reina.

I opened my eyes and peered up at where I imagined Mraugathal's face might be.

The Eldervine went quiet, as though thinking.

Finally, his leaves rustled. *Ah. Yes. Yes, we sense them. We sense* all *of them.*

Relief rushed through me. "You do?" I tried to contain the hope swelling in my chest. "Do you know where they are?"

Mraugathal's voice grew grave. *You may not be happy with what I show you.*

The hope gave way to dread. But they were alive, right, if he could sense them? Or could he sense them even if—I shoved away my mounting panic. Whatever the truth was, I needed to know. "Show me." My voice trembled. "Please."

The world around me fell away as Mraugathal's visions filled my mind.

# CHAPTER 21

# THE FINAL STROKE

*Jordan*

Sevryn glared at us, holding up the note Etcher had pulled from the vial.

"I found it in the faespell," Etcher hurried to explain, "not sure what—"

"Don't lie to me!" Sevryn yelled. "Your time is up. You will cure the king *right now,* or all *three* of you will go to the gallows!"

I edged closer to Madison, hoping to protect her if things went south, though I didn't want to move too far from Etcher, either, in case he needed me.

"Be reasonable," Etcher said. "I can't craft a rune in that short of—"

"*Reasonable*? I've already arrested the apothecarist—one of my men in the city overheard him talking about your visit. You were planning to *kill* me?" He let out a harsh laugh. "Part of me would've liked to see you try. I don't care what Beirthyr thought about your so-called 'loyal' reputation; I should've had you executed the moment I found out you were a LeyGuard."

Sevryn glanced at the four guards standing in the hall. "You, take the supplies, all of them. You three, grab the prisoners!"

One guard rushed in and scooped armfuls of the Runing supplies into a basket without much care for damaging them. The other three guards swept in and grabbed each of us by the arms.

"Ow, you're hurting me!" Madison cried out.

"Ease up." I glared at the guard.

He adjusted his grip on her arm slightly, but not by much.

They dragged us out into the hallway and through the corridors toward Beirthyr's chambers.

The guards shoved all three of us into Beirthyr's room and plunked our basket of supplies on the bench at the foot of Beirthyr's curtained bed.

"Cure him," Sevryn growled. "And don't try a single thing else." He removed both Etcher's and my rune-cuffs, though the guards stayed within reach of us. "Last chance to stay alive." He sank into the chair at Beirthyr's mirrored vanity, glaring at us from the corner.

Should we try to escape? Would it do any good? Etcher knew these men better, understood more of the risks. I glanced at him, waiting for his lead.

Etcher rubbed his wrist where the guard had none-too-gently yanked his cuff free, then grabbed a quill and a vial of ink from the basket. He dipped the quill and returned the vial, then yanked open the bed's curtains.

Beirthyr looked even more awful than the last time we'd seen him—his skin was jaundiced and clammy, his eyes puffy, his cheeks sunken, and his breaths were fast and shallow.

Etcher had apparently decided to do as told. He shoved up Beirthyr's loose sleeve and immediately began sketching a rune.

Madison moved up close behind me, as far as she could get from Sevryn and his guards.

After a few quick strokes, I recognized the rune Etcher was drawing—a mind-sifter rune. I sucked a quick breath. Etcher was staying true to his word, making sure Beirthyr wasn't an innocent victim before we went any further.

Etcher pulled me forward and placed his free hand on my forearm, then dragged my hand onto Beirthyr's forehead.

Sevryn rose to his feet in the corner. "What are you doing?"

"A sensing rune," Etcher said. "The boy must wield it while I complete the inking, but it will allow us to see the state of our patient's condition."

Etcher made the final stroke, and a surge of panic and pain rushed into my mind, along with a deep voice that must've been Beirthyr's. *Kill him! Find Kaizyn. Kill me if you must, but stop the Selkblood!*

I yanked my hand away. Etcher slid his hand from my forearm, but from his glance, I knew he'd heard it, too.

Etcher started to rune something on Beirthyr again, then turned to Sevryn. "I cannot guarantee this will work. I haven't had time to—"

"Just *do* it!" Sevryn growled.

Etcher sucked a sharp breath, then runed something I could only partially recognize—a mix of the marks for fire, serpent, free will, and... something else I couldn't interpret.

Etcher glanced back at me. "Get ready to wield it."

I tightened my grip on the energy within me that controlled my fire magic, and tensed, ready to move quickly if needed.

Etcher made the final stroke—a mark of binding—and his eyes locked on me. "*Now.*"

I slapped my hand over the rune and shoved my magic into it.

Fire surged through me. A shout of pain escaped me as the rune's magic set my veins aflame.

Etcher jumped back as Beirthyr seized, his body surging with a hot glow.

Beirthyr's chest exploded in a slithering torrent of flame.

I yanked my hand away and stumbled back, taking Madison with me.

"The fire-serpent!" The guards yelled, fleeing for the door as the flame seared through the bed's canopy.

"Hold your position!" Sevryn screamed, but they ignored him and rushed out into the hall.

The spewing column of flame from Beirthyr's chest intensified.

Sevryn stalked toward Etcher and me, his glare burning into us. "What have you *done*?"

Madison yelped and pressed herself into my back.

Etcher straightened and met Sevryn's glare with a glare of his own. "I've broken your hold on Beirthyr's mind. His body might be too far gone to fight you, but the fire-serpent *you* tried to trap inside him is not."

Sevryn's eyes widened in surprise, just as the column of fire looped itself back around and turned a fiery snake-face toward Sevryn. Its smoldering-coal eyes locked on Sevryn as its flaming tongue flickered in and out.

It coiled to leap—

"*Enough!*" Sevryn swung his hands wide, and I felt his power grab me. I dangled, immobile, in the grip of his Selkblood control... just as I'd feared when I first faced him in the prison.

I could move my eyes only enough to see that Etcher was in the same state, and judging from its sudden lack of motion, so was the fire-serpent. I assumed Madison was, as well. Sevryn had seized us all like puppets in an instant, and even with the rune cuff off, my magic was no match for him. Every time I tried to grip my magic, Sevryn's control punched it back, and it slid right out of my grasp.

Sevryn stalked closer with an angry sneer. "Did you think this little stunt would actually *work*? That some pesky fire-serpent would ride in and *save* you?"

The serpent began moving again, but in circles in the air, as though disoriented.

"Did you think Beirthyr *himself* never tried that?" Sevryn laughed. "Serpents hunt by sensing the air—they are extremely sensitive to changes in scents, in the chemicals that control sensation and even emotion, in *pheromones*...one of the very things we Selkbloods specialize in." His sneer spread into a grin that sent a chill down my spine. "No simple fire-serpent could ever pose a threat to me."

He waved a finger, and the fire-serpent went still again.

"I'm tired of this charade," Sevryn hissed. "Tired of jumping through all of Teionyr's magical hoops. The Dark King grows impatient with diplomacy."

*The Dark King*? Did the Selkbloods have a monarch at the head of all their chaos? I filed that away to look into later, but I certainly didn't like the sound of it.

"You call what you've done here *diplomatic*?" Etcher barked, though his voice was strained.

Sevryn spun to him. "I haven't killed anyone yet, have I? Well, other than the handful of guards who were foolish enough to spew treason against Beirthyr, but he ordered their executions himself."

"Under *your* influence," Etcher said.

Sevryn ignored him. "I tried to negotiate a deal for sharing this city's resources, to come at this peacefully…" He turned to glare at Beirthyr. "And it was going rather well until *he* began resisting." He spun back around to Etcher and me with a smile that sent ice down my spine. "You've done me a favor by freeing Beirthyr's mind: You've shown me he's truly worthless to me. I can see his thoughts clearly again, now that he's done resisting me. If he ever did have the information I needed, it's long gone. He's useless."

He snarled the last word as he lunged for Beirthyr's bed.

"No!" I jumped to stop him—but my jump got me nowhere; Sevryn's grip still held me in place.

I watched with sickening helplessness as Sevryn grabbed Beirthyr's head and snapped his neck.

The fire-serpent stiffened, then its flames winked out. It thunked to the bed on top of Beirthyr, its body now a lifeless, dull brown.

Sevryn spun toward me. "Our deal is off. The time for negotiation has passed."

Guards rushed in from the hall, different ones than before. "Summon my brothers and their darklings," Sevryn told them. "Teionyr has resources the Dark King wants. If I can't seize them the peaceful way, I'll have to take them by force."

Sevryn lunged around me and grabbed Madison by the arm.

She screamed. "Let go of me!"

Everything in my body shouted for me to help her, but Sevryn's power still held me in an iron grip. My words were all I had, and even those took an effort to get out against the grip of his magic. "Let her go! She had nothing to do with this."

Sevryn sneered at me, then shoved Madison at the guards. "Bind her tighter."

"You coward!" I fought Sevryn's hold with *everything* I had, and his grip slipped just enough that my fist broke free and sailed straight into the side of Sevryn's face.

A guard slugged me in the nose in return.

My hard-fought control snapped like a broken rubber band as Sevryn's power clamped back over me with such vengeance, I could barely move my eyes.

Hot liquid poured from my broken nose, but I still got satisfaction from seeing Sevryn spit blood.

"You'll *pay* for that," he growled as his glare burned into me.

"And *you* are a coward"—I paused; every word took such effort—"who gets twisted pleasure out of hurting and scaring women who have done *nothing* to threaten you. Hasn't Madison suffered *enough* because of you?"

Sevryn stepped so close I could feel his horrid, hot breath on my face. "You haven't known the *meaning* of suffering until today." He pulled back. "Guards, take them to the gallows, and summon the crowds." He stalked toward the door, then shot a cold grin back at us over his shoulder. "It's time for an execution."

# CHAPTER 22

# THE RIGHT HUMANS

*Ayla*

The area in front of Keyja's cottage faded away as Mraugathal pushed an image into my mind of a steep cliff with a sheer drop-off into darkness below and nothing but open sky around it, save for a handful of bats swarming around something on the side of the cliff.

The image was fuzzy, at first, then it clarified. Those weren't bats — they were much too big, each the size of a large dog, and *horrid*, with long, bony arms that clawed and shoved, beating their wings against each other as they tried to get at whatever they were swarming on the cliff face.

Their intended meal, whatever it was, seemed to be fighting back—I could hear squeals of pain as it lashed out at the creatures, barely keeping them at bay. As they fought and shifted, I got a glimpse of what they were after.

"Oh no." It was *Reina*.

Her red hair was matted to her forehead with blood, and she was banged up and filthy, like she'd just climbed up from a mud pit, but it was definitely her. She clung to a small outcropping on the cliff, jabbing at the creatures with a dagger in one hand, then clambering for holds to climb higher as the creatures regrouped.

I could see what she was trying to make it to—the shimmering surface of a LeyGate opening glistened at the top of the cliff.

My heart soared as I spotted Champ there beside it, dancing anxiously at the edge as he peered down at Reina. But the way those creatures were swooping in and jabbing at her, I didn't see how she could make it up to Champ and the LeyGate before the creatures knocked her grip loose.

I shook my head, trying to clear the vision. "Please. We have to help her!"

"What did you see?" I heard Callan ask, but before I could answer, Mraugathal spoke into my mind again.

*Wait. I must show you more.*

The cliff vanished, replaced by a dirt-floored, open-air courtyard lined with colorful tents—some kind of town square. People milled about, still fuzzy in the vision, though they clustered mostly around something at the center of the square. My throat tightened as the vision cleared and I saw what they were gathered around: gallows. Four of them, set up right in the middle of the square. One of them already had a man on it, held in place by an armed guard, though the man wasn't anyone I recognized. My pulse quickened. Was he a criminal? Why was Mraugathal showing me this?

Guards shoved through the crowded square, leading some kind of procession. The crowds parted in a hurry—and my breath caught. *Sevryn.* I would recognize those cold, blue eyes anywhere. He strode through the square like he owned the place, guards flanking him and more guards trailing behind him, dragging three limp and bloodied prisoners. One was an older man, somewhere between my parents' and grandfather's age. My heart lurched for him. Then the other two prisoners came into better view: a blonde girl and—*No. Oh, please God, no.* I prayed I was wrong, but as the guards dragged them out of the crowd and shoved them toward the gallows, there was no mistaking their bloodied faces.

The other two were Madison and Jordan.

I screamed.

The vision snapped away, and instantly Callan's arms were on mine, holding me upright. "What is it, Ayla? What did you see?"

"They're going to hang them." I forced my eyes up to his, then glanced at Rory. "They're going to *hang* Jordan and Madison."

"*What?*" Rory's face blanched. He buried his hands in his short hair. "No—that can't be right—we have to do something!

"How recent are these visions, Mraugathal?" Callan's voice was sharp, edged with panic.

*This moment. It is happening right now, in Teionyr.*

"Why didn't you tell us sooner?" I yelled at the giant celery. "They're leading them to the gallows—we have minutes, at most!"

*I showed as my cousins saw,* Mraugathal answered in my mind. *We were not even sure we had the right humans until you confirmed.*

He must have spoken that to Keyja, too, because I heard her repeating the explanation to Callan—but I was swinging between shock and panic.

"Please. *Please.*" I stared up at Mraugathal. "We have to help them." I looked at the others. "And Reina was climbing for a LeyGate; dark, flying creatures were attacking her—"

Mraugathal's leaves rustled as he spoke further. *That human seems to be getting the better of the darklings. She is almost to the top of the cliff, now. Your friends in the square are still being led by the Selkblood. They are almost through the crowds.*

I relayed his words to the others. "We'll have to hope Reina can make it on her own. Jordan and Madison are almost to the gallows." The words stuck in my throat.

Rory moved up beside me. "Ayla, *please,* there has to be something we can—"

I turned to Keyja. "How long does it take to get to Teionyr? We have to help them!"

Callan's eyes widened in despair. "They're in Teionyr? We'll never make it in time." He spun to Keyja. "Is there *anything* you can do?"

Keyja looked as despairing as the rest of us. "No, I don't think so—I'm sorry, I wish I could, but I cannot transport anyone, and there are no direct passages that could take us to Teionyr; their magic prevents direct access to outsiders. Even with Tofa's help, it would take hours for me to get from here to there... There's no way I could get you there in time." Her eyes welled up. "I'm truly sorry."

"No." I said the word with authority that surprised even me. Everyone turned to stare at me. "*No.* This is *not* how it ends." I didn't care *how* we got to Teionyr, we were going. Even if we got there too late, even if it killed us, we were going to try. "We are *not* just going to sit here and—"

"Keyja can't get you there," a familiar voice said, "but I can."

A doorway peeled open in the air near Keyja's cottage, framing Kaizyn in the darkness beyond. He was pale and panting—the door must have extracted its price again.

His gaze locked on me from where he stood. "Ayla, please, I can help. Teionyrian royals have direct access to Teionyr—from anywhere. I can travel to Teionyr in a single moment, if I wish. I haven't been able to use it, not with the curse, because if I leave the Veil, I die. But—"

Before I could respond, Callan stepped between us.

"You just said, if you leave the Veil, you *die!*" He lowered his voice. "Why are you even—you're supposed to be somewhere safe!"

Kaizyn glanced at me again before answering Callan. "I stayed close, and I felt Ayla's fear. I heard the rest as I was opening the door. Please, let me help."

"You *can't!*" Callan shoved his hands into his hair. "Leaving the Veil will kill you! With the bond, it will kill you *both!*"

Fear flickered in Kaizyn's eyes.

Callan's face softened. "I know you want to help, but—"

Keyja interrupted. "There is a way." She locked eyes with Kaizyn, and an understanding passed between them. "But she must know what she is choosing."

"Of course." Kaizyn looked insulted. "I would not allow it any other way."

Keyja nodded. "Very well." She turned to me, speaking urgently. "I cannot break his curse, but... if one is bonded tightly enough, their life can sustain the life of another, even against a curse such as this one. Such a one could even travel instantly into Teionyr with a royal, because to the magic, the two would be bound so tightly, they are one and the same. The same way his sear-bind travels with him."

I stared at her. "What are you saying?"

Her gaze held mine. "The prince can take you to Teionyr, Ayla. You and he and Vyrthil could be there within moments, and your life-force will allow Kaizyn to leave the Veil, despite the curse. But only if you allow me to bind you to Kaizyn, body and soul."

I glanced at Kaizyn. "We're already bound!... Aren't we?"

Kaizyn's cheeks reddened, and the discomfort on his face only intensified my anxiety. "Not like this, Ayla. This will bind your *energy* to mine, not just our lives. Your very energy will sustain my life, and vice versa. When one of us tires or gets sick, the other immediately will, too. You will feel my emotions, not just me feeling yours. Everything the bond has already done will be intensified. We will be entwined. There *is* no closer bond through magic."

Kaizyn glanced away, then forced his eyes back to mine. "And... it would be permanent."

I gaped at him. *Permanent?* We could reach Jordan in time, try to save him, but even if we succeeded... I would be bound even more deeply to Kaizyn... *forever.*

Vyrthil stalked up behind Kaizyn in the Veil beyond the doorway.

Kaizyn's eyes locked on mine, pleading. "I still have my magic, Ayla. And you have yours. We will have the element of surprise, and I'm a trained warrior." He held up his hands, flames dancing on his fingertips.

Between that and the sword at his waist and Vyrthil standing guard beside him, he looked every bit the Fae warrior he claimed to be.

He stepped closer, to the very edge of the doorway. "I will do my best to save Jordan and Madison for you, Ayla. I *want* to help you. But—to my knowledge, there's no way to undo this entwining. You and I would be bound *forever.* Do you understand? I need you to be sure."

My brain glitched as I realized what this meant, and Kaizyn's face softened.

"I wish with everything in me that you didn't have to make this choice," he said, "and especially that you didn't have to make it so quickly. But, Ayla—this is the only way I know to help, and I fear we are running out of time. If we hope to save your friends, Keyja needs to conduct the binding *now*."

He was right. Heaven help me, he was right. It terrified me to bond myself to Kaizyn even further—I'd be a fool to think I could ever have a relationship outside of Kaizyn, while entwined with him like that. Which meant Jordan and I—

I sucked a sharp breath. This choice felt like an internal death. But if I did nothing, Jordan and Madison would die an *actual* death, and I couldn't just let them die. Not when I might be able to save them.

I met Kaizyn's gaze. Pain flashed in his eyes as my care for Madison and my love for Jordan rushed through the bond we *already* shared, along with regret and a faint twinge of guilt. I didn't feel for Kaizyn the way he felt for me. I never would've chosen this otherwise, and I knew he could feel that. He could feel everything.

"You understand why I would be doing this?" I asked him.

"Yes," he said. "I know. But what matters to you, matters to me. I want to help."

Resolve settled in my heart, along with a stab of pain as the finality of my choice sank in. A bond like this would mean the end of any chance for a romantic relationship with Jordan. But at least, if we succeeded, Jordan and Madison would be alive.

I turned to Keyja. "Do it."

# CHAPTER 23
# THE TRUE HEIR OF TEIONYR

*Striker*

Brone met me as I stepped through the Hub entrance. He wore a clean set of LeyGuard battle leathers, his signature pistol on his belt, and his face and stance were tense.

"We've got a problem." He waved for me to follow, then jogged across the Hub courtyard toward the stairs.

I jogged behind him. "So I gathered."

A few of the Hub staff cast glances our way as we rushed up the stairs to the landing.

I was sure they wondered where I'd been—I had disappeared around the same time as Ayla and Reina and Callan, and the Hub would have noticed their absence by now.

It was only a matter of time before Chairman Hart got word I was here and came to interrogate me, but if Brone had something he needed to show me, that's where I would go. Chairman Hart could track me down herself.

When we reached the top of the stairs, Brone glanced around, then kept his voice low. "Are the girl and the prince safe?"

"For now. They're with Keyja."

Brone huffed a sigh of relief. "Good, because things here have hit the fan. C'mon."

He hurried toward the med room where I'd last seen Maddox Rogers and hit the button to open the door. I followed him in.

I was relieved to see Maddox resting peacefully in the bed. I turned to Brone as he closed the door behind us. "What's this about? Something wrong with the old man? Ayla's parents?"

Brone laughed nervously—that alone made me tense. Not even an army of Fadehounds could make Brone nervous.

"No," he said. "Girl's parents are the same, and Maddox is fine. It's what he's *remembered* that's the problem."

I stared at him. "What do you—"

The Hub sirens blared the breach alarm.

Brone and I met wide stares, then raced for the door.

We leaped down the steps several at a time as Chairman Hart's voice echoed through the overhead speakers above the deafening sirens: "Possible Class One Breach. I repeat, possible Class One Breach. All LeyGuards report to the—"

Just as Brone and I hit the bottom floor, a LeyGate split open across the courtyard.

A girl staggered through, filthy and bloody, holding the limp, gashed-up body of a large dog.

"*Reina?*" Footsteps and chaos sounded all around me as I rushed forward to help her.

Brone hurried up next to me and gently slid Champ from Reina's grip as I steadied her. Her body was trembling.

Her eyes locked on mine in panic. "Darklings after Kaizyn. A whole army. Sevryn has Jordan!"

She collapsed in my arms.

I scooped her up.

Chairman Hart fell in step behind me as I rushed Reina toward the med corridor.

"Striker. Striker!" Chairman Hart called after me, but I ignored her.

"He's trying to help one of our own, Meredith. Get off his back!" Brone shouted from close behind me.

Brone's words would come back to bite him later, but for now they did the trick.

Hart stopped at the landing and yelled after us. "Fine! But both of you will report to me as soon as she's settled!"

The moment I stepped foot in the med room, Doctor Harlowe rushed to meet me.

"Put her here, put the dog there." He pointed out two empty examination tables. "The rest of you, out!"

Brone set Champ on the designated table, then stepped back toward the door.

I lowered Reina to the other table and glanced back to see we'd accumulated a small crowd of nosy LeyGuard staff at the door.

Brone held them back. "Give them room!"

Two figures shoved through. "Reina. Reina!" The crowd parted and let them in—Reina's parents.

Reina had always been a feisty trainee, more than capable for her age, but no kid that age should have to go through the type of experience Reina's beat-up face and body indicated.

I stepped back as Reina's parents rushed to her side, then I turned to Doctor Harlowe, who was digging out handfuls of runestones from a metal drawer. "Will she be okay?"

He glanced at Reina's parents, then looked up at me. "I appreciate your help getting her to me quickly, but I have to ask you to leave now. Confidentiality."

I nodded. "Of course."

The crowd at the door had dispersed, and I could hear Chairman Hart barking orders in the hall.

Reina's mother grabbed my arm as I slid past. Her gaze met mine. "Thank you."

I nodded again, then followed Brone out into the hall.

Chairman Hart was waiting for us with a frosty glare. "Both of you, in my office. Now."

She ushered us down the hall to her office, then slammed the door and sank into her desk chair.

At her gesture, Brone and I plopped into the two armchairs opposite her.

Brone cut his eyes to me as Chairman Hart glared at us across her desk—I knew he still had information to tell me about whatever Maddox Rogers had remembered, probably information he didn't want to say in front of Chairman Hart. It would have to wait.

"Well?" Chairman Hart snapped. "I hope you two have an explanation."

I leaned back in my chair and stretched my arms out on the armrests, letting Brone take the lead.

"You'll have to be more specific than that, Meredith," Brone said, his voice deadpan. "A lot has happened the past few days."

I fought back a smirk. Brone was the *only* one at the Hub who dared call Hart by her first name in an official setting—Hart was his late wife's sister, so he could get away with it. Barely. Telling her to get off my back in the hallway, though... not so much. That alone would've been enough to set Hart fuming, and we'd done *a lot* more.

Hart's face turned a shade of red that signaled incoming disaster. Her glare settled on me. "Explain to me why you helped a group of LeyGuard *trainees* breach Faeside during an emergency Hub lockdown. How about we start there?" Her words hung in the air like icicles, hard and frosty.

I held her gaze. "They would've gone, anyway. I just did my best to make sure they didn't get themselves killed."

Her glare deepened. "Why didn't you just *report* them? The council was making plans for the retrieval of Jordan Peters, and—"

Brone slapped his hands on Hart's desk, startling us both. "We don't have *time* for this, Meredith!" He ran a hand through his hair, then turned to me. I trusted Brone with my life, but his nerves were back, which didn't do so well for nerves of my own.

"Brone?"

He huffed. "He said not to say it in front of—but whatever, there's no time. Kaizyn is *not* the crown prince of Teionyr."

Hart and I both gaped at him. "*What?*"

Brone nodded. "Maddox Rogers woke up extremely lucid for a brief period, and in that time, he dropped a bomb on me—Kaizyn isn't the prince at all. Jordan Peters is."

I stared at him as that sank in. "How is that possible?"

His words came out in a rush. "The day the Dark Fae attacked the palace, and the queen went into labor, Maddox swapped the infant prince with a servant's baby as part of his promise to the queen to protect the heir. She'd had a vision of something bad coming. They sealed the prince's Fae magic with a blood spell from the dying queen and Maddox brought him Earthside in guise as an orphaned LeyGuard infant. The Peters adopted him. The servant mother died in the attack, and few but the queen and Maddox ever knew what really happened. I'm not even sure the king knew. Maddox hid the prince's true name somewhere in Teionyr. It's the only thing that can break the blood spell and release his Fae magic. The riddle, the true name, it was never really about Kaizyn at all."

Hart's face went pale. "That makes Jordan the true heir of Teionyr."

Brone nodded. "Yes. The Teionyrian magic must already be destabilizing—Kaizyn was never meant to wield it. Even though he was marked with the Seal at his presentation ceremony as an infant, he's not the rightful heir. Usually, that ceremony is just for show; the Seal binds to the royal bloodline automatically. A seated royal can place the Seal on an adopted family member, but that wouldn't take the place of the bloodline connection that stabilizes the kingdom's magic, without additional ceremonies—which Veilar either didn't know to do, or didn't do for the sake of keeping up the ruse. It's no wonder Sevryn and his men infiltrated the city so easily after King Veilar's death."

I turned to Hart. "Then it's only a matter of time until the wards around the palace vault weaken, too. If Sevryn figures that out, he'll have access to the most powerful cache of magical resources in all of Upper Faeside. All he has to do is wait it out. Do you think he knows?"

Brone shook his head. "Maddox wasn't sure. But we also have another problem. The Seal won't protect Jordan, not with his Fae magic bound. Until that's undone, he can be killed as easily as anyone else. If Sevryn really has Jordan, like Reina said…"

I met his stare. "He could kill the true heir to Teionyr's throne, whether he *knows* that's what he's doing or not. You know what that could mean?"

Chairman Hart rose to her feet. "We've been protecting the wrong prince." She leaned forward, supporting herself against her desk with shaky arms. "The rescue I delayed might very well decide the entire war."

Brone and I both stood. I stepped toward Hart. "We have to get to Teionyr."

"Yes." She nodded, then shook her head. "But no, we can't—I mean, I suspect there may be someone on the Hub council reporting back to the Selkbloods."

Brone tensed. "*What*? Who?"

"I don't know. But the information, the coincidences… it's too much to ignore. That's why I waited. I was trying to investigate…" Her eyes widened. "We can't tell the council this. Any of it. We'll have to send a covert team."

"You mean Striker and me, obviously." Brone raised an eyebrow. "Who else can you trust?"

The door shoved open. "I'm going with you."

Brone and I both spun toward the door.

Maddox Rogers stood in the doorway, wearing old-school battle leathers instead of his hospital gown. A worn leather weapons belt hung at his waist, battle knives tucked in the sheaths on either side. Where had he dug *those* up? He looked none-too-steady on his feet.

"I'm going with you," he said again. "I have… a key. A way directly into the city. A back entrance set up by the queen herself."

"How did you get in here, Maddox?" Hart's tone was respectful, which was more than I expected, given how unsettled she looked by his presence. "I specifically told my assistants—"

"*We* let him in." Jordan's parents stepped up behind him, also wearing full battle leathers along with their weapons of choice: a belt with a dagger for Jordan's mother and a bow and quiver for his father. I'd had limited interaction with them among the LeyGuard. They were Valos, but Tier B fire-wielders—which meant their fire magic wasn't as strong as their weapons skills. They used fire only as a backup, not as their primary attack like mine.

"You're going after Jordan, right?" Jordan's dad faced Hart like a warrior, shoulders back, firm gaze unflinching. "We're going, too."

Hart's gaze locked on his. "Did you hear what—"

"Maddox just told us," Jordan's mother said. "But we don't care. Ley-Guard or Fae, he's our *son*."

Hart sighed. "Fine." She turned to Maddox Rogers. "But Maddox, they decommissioned you years ago. And you're not... well. I can't allow—"

"I have to go." Maddox straightened and gripped the handles of his knives. His glare locked on Hart, and for a moment, he looked every bit the LeyGuard hero he used to be. "It's *my* key. Besides, this was my mission, *my* promise to keep, and I will finish this." He narrowed a glare at her. "Try to stop me."

Old man had nerve, I'd give him that. I fought back a grin as he and Hart glared at each other.

"He's going." Reina's voice from the hallway interrupted their staring match as Reina walked up behind Maddox. She had been treated and cleaned up, and though bruising splotched her face and she had a couple bandaged spots on her forehead, that feisty energy was back in her eyes. She wore battle leathers with her sword at her waist.

Jordan's dog, Champ, sidled up behind Reina, already wearing his canine armor. Other than some scratches and a bandage around one foreleg, he seemed fine.

Her parents stepped up behind her, also dressed in battle gear. "So are we."

Hart let out a noisy sigh and rubbed her forehead. "My word, it's like someone sent out a party invitation."

I smiled at Reina. "Good to see you up and moving, kid."

She stared past me for a moment, looking slightly dazed. "I can't believe Jordan is a..." But then she shook her head and addressed Hart directly. "I didn't get to finish my report. My Faeside sources say Sevryn plans to hang Jordan in the square *tonight*. He doesn't seem to know Jordan's true identity. Jordan's execution is a trap to lure in Ayla and Kaizyn. He also has Madison Kane, and he plans to kill all four, plus Callan too, if he shows up. Sevryn has a darkling army hidden in the mountains around Teionyr."

My eyebrows shot up. Impressive intel for a kid on the run in the Void, but Reina had always been skilled at spy craft.

Hart cursed under her breath. "We may already be too late."

"Not if we go now," Reina said. "When I came through, they were just assembling the crowds and getting things ready. We could still make it. We have to try."

Hart's gaze softened with compassion as Reina spoke, but she still looked hesitant.

"With all due respect, Chairman," Jordan's father said, "most of us plan to go whether you authorize it or not. It would save a lot of time if you didn't try to stop us."

Hart glanced around at the seven of us—eight, if you included Champ. She sighed again. "Go. But do it quickly and quietly. I'll think of something to tell the council to keep them off your track." She met my eyes, then Brone's. "Striker, you're the mission leader. Brone, you're his second."

Brone grinned at me—we knew our roles well. "Ready to go save a kingdom and some kids?"

I glanced over my motley assortment of a mission team—four adult Ley-Guards, two of whom were still beat up from their run-in with Selkbloods at the warehouse docks, one LeyGuard trainee fresh off a trip back from the Void, and a crazy retiree. Every single one of their faces contained the battle spark—the one that said they would die for this cause. That, plus Brone and me and an armored dog? What better comrades could I have asked for?

I stuck a fresh match in the side of my mouth. "All right, team. Let's go."

# CHAPTER 24

# LET'S PLAY

***Ayla***

The orb in Keyja's chest crackled with electricity as she stepped up next to Kaizyn and me. "Grab hands, quickly."

Kaizyn held his palms out, still outside the doorway, and I reached across the threshold and placed my hands in his.

Keyja moved next to me and grabbed our joined hands with both of hers, clamping them together. "You will feel a hum, then a hot buzz. Do *not* remove your hands."

I nodded, then glanced back at Kaizyn. His deep blue eyes locked with mine. "I'm sorry, Ayla. I know you didn't want this."

I stared back, unsure how to respond—then Keyja's electricity surged through our joined hands.

Crackling fire rushed through my veins. Every muscle tensed, my head flew back.

And then, like a tidal wave slamming into me, I felt... *Kaizyn.*

His concern for me, his care for me, his worry and his guilt and his fears. The sheer intensity of it took my breath away.

I came up gasping as Keyja's magic pulled back and found those deep blue eyes locked on mine again.

For a moment, the raw force of Kaizyn's emotions toward me paralyzed me. I stared back at him. "I didn't know."

*Truly, I didn't know.* I never imagined what he felt for me was like this.

"I'm sorry," he whispered, and I felt the violent crash of that, too—regret, concern, fear that I would hate him for this, that I would blame him, especially if we failed to save Jordan.

He pulled his hands away. "We need to go."

He hesitated only a moment, then stepped through the doorway into Arcvale.

"Kaizyn—" Callan called out, but to everyone's relief, nothing bad happened.

Kaizyn grabbed my hands again, then muttered foreign words, and the air in front of us split open into a swirling vortex of darkness.

A few weeks ago, I wouldn't have imagined that *anything* could have convinced me to leap headlong through a Fae portal into the dark and dangerous unknown of the Void. But now, as I prepared to plummet into the Void for the third time in a matter of days, I realized just how many reasons I had to brave this danger. Grandpa. My parents. Reina, Callan, Madison, Rory, Champ, even Striker and Kaizyn. I would risk this for any of them... and I had. But Jordan—oh, Jordan. I would leap into the Void a million times over, if I knew for sure it would save him. My love and concern for him surged in fierce and raw, making my chest clench.

Kaizyn's immediate, brokenhearted response—a fierce surge of sorrow tinged with jealousy—hit me like a shock wave.

I gasped, completely disoriented by it. It wasn't his fault; I knew that—he felt what he felt. It was just... overwhelming. And more than a little confusing. I sucked a slow breath, shaking myself back into focus. "Go. We need to go."

Kaizyn was trying to stuff his feelings down; I could feel that, too—but he just felt so *much*, it was hard to think straight through it.

"How do you *do* this?" I asked him. Had he been living like this, this whole time, feeling my every emotion this intensely on top of his own?

Kaizyn stepped toward me. "I'm sorry," he whispered again, and I felt how deeply he meant it. "Hold on tight."

He wrapped his arms around me and he, Vyrthil, and I were sucked into the Void.

*Please God, please,* I prayed as I hurtled into the darkness. *Don't let us be too late.*

The trip was shockingly short. The darkness split open mere seconds later. Kaizyn and I crashed to our knees on a packed-dirt surface, blinking against the harsh sun.

We had dropped right in the middle of a crowded market square.

The surrounding people gasped and jumped back.

I glanced up through the crowd, and my heart stuttered—there was Jordan, chained to the gallows, a rope around his neck. *Still alive.* A shuddering breath of relief rushed through me—then caught in my throat. A Fae guard next to him gripped a lever, connected to the trap-door on the gallows floor that could drop Jordan to his death.

Madison and the old man I'd seen in the vision were secured on gallows to either side of Jordan, each with another guard and lever. And on the far end was the other old man, also chained up for a hanging and accompanied by a guard.

The crowd hovered around the gallows, and for a moment, I just stared at them. How could they all just *watch* this?

Reality caught up to me, and I scrambled to my feet. "Jordan. Jordan!"

His head flicked toward me. One of his eyes was blackened and swollen shut, but the other searched the crowd. "Ayla?"

Around us, gasps and whispers broke out as Kaizyn pushed to his feet. "The prince. It's the prince!"

A cold laugh cut through the murmur. "Ayla Rogers."

The crowd fell into a tense silence.

Sevryn stepped out of the crowd with an icy grin. "We meet again. Ah! And you brought your prince. How thoughtful of you."

*Magic.* I needed to use my magic. Fear snaked through me as I grasped for it, but though I could feel a strange coldness churning inside me, I couldn't get a hold on it.

A swell of fierce, protective fury joined that fear as Kaizyn stepped up next to me, Vyrthil blazing at his side. "Stay away from her."

His confidence washed in over me, calming the panic.

"You can do this, Ayla." Kaizyn leaned next to my ear. "I'm right here with you."

The cold power within me solidified into something I could grasp, and I clenched onto it for dear life, unsure how to use it or what might happen next.

"Ayla?" Jordan called for me again.

My voice broke as I answered him. "I'm here. We're here. Just hold on!"

Worry washed over Jordan's bloodied face as he searched the crowd for me, sweeping away the joy that had popped up first. "Run, Ayla. Get out of here. Run!"

All around the square, shadowy, bat-like shapes appeared on the tops of the buildings and walls. *Darklings.* Like I'd seen in my vision of Reina.

Kaizyn stepped in front of me as guards moved toward us.

"Oh, so soon?" Sevryn called. "But we were just beginning to have fun!" He raised a hand, and the guards on the gallows platforms all reached for their levers.

"No!" I screamed, but then the guards spun, all in unison—and cut the ropes.

Madison, Jordan, and the two other men dropped to their knees on the gallows platform.

Sevryn turned in a slow circle, gesturing to the crowd. "You came here for a show?" He grinned, but then he turned to me and Kaizyn, and his glare was like ice. "Let's *play.*"

He swung his hands upward, and Jordan and Madison both went rigid, then flew down from the platforms like puppets yanked by strings.

Jordan flailed and fought against Sevryn's hold, but he was under the Selkblood's control.

Madison's chest heaved, her eyes flicking back and forth in panic.

The crowds scattered back as Sevryn lowered Jordan and Madison to the ground near him, just beyond arms' reach of Kaizyn and me.

Guards slid in around Sevryn, blocking him from us, leaving me to stare at Madison and Jordan. *Jordan.* Our gazes locked for the first time in what felt like forever.

For a moment, the panic in his one good eye softened into pure affection. His hand twitched, as though reaching for me—then it slammed back against his side.

"Ah ah ah," Sevryn said. "Be a good puppet and do what you're *told!*"

Sevryn swung his hand, and flames shot from Jordan's fingertips.

"Nooo!" Jordan yelled like something had ripped the sound from his chest as Kaizyn shoved me out of the way.

I hit the ground hard, and Kaizyn landed beside me. His body had taken the brunt of the flame. Part of his tunic hung charred, revealing his muscled torso beneath, but he seemed otherwise unharmed.

The darklings around the tops of the walls squirmed, watching us.

Kaizyn helped me to my feet.

When I looked back at Jordan, his stare was pure agony. "Run, Ayla. Please! Ru—" His word cut off as though strangled, and again his hands shot up. "*No!*"

This time, he seemed to fight Sevryn's hold, at least for a moment. The flames flickered in and out, then Sevryn's control won out and a torrent of fire shot out from Jordan's hands in our direction.

The delay had given Kaizyn and me time to move; the flames hit the ground near our feet.

"I can't fight fire with fire, Ayla," Kaizyn whispered from beside me. His concern surged through our bond, followed by a wave of confidence. "But you have ice. See if you can slow him, distract him. Fight back enough to keep his attention on you and Jordan, and please, keep yourself alive. Vyrthil and I will try to get to Sevryn."

Jordan was resisting again, twitching against Sevryn's control a few yards from me.

I gripped the cold power inside me as I stared at Jordan. "Will it hurt him?"

I felt Kaizyn's hesitation. "I—I don't know." He gripped my arm, and I turned to find his intense blue eyes staring at me. "But Ayla, you *have* to know he'd rather you hurt him a little to protect yourself, than for his magic to be used to harm you. Look at him. He's in agony."

A complex wave of emotion accompanied Kaizyn's statement, but I was too preoccupied with Sevryn and Jordan to process it.

Jordan's eyes were locked on mine, begging me to run.

"Okay," I whispered, steeling myself. *Keep myself alive, keep Sevryn distracted.* I could use my ice, fend off the fire until Kaizyn could get to Sevryn—maybe sting Jordan, but not harm him. I could do that, right? I had to. Otherwise, we might *all* be dead.

Sevryn slashed his hand through the air again, and Jordan let out a strangled yell—but this time, I was ready.

A surge of icy magic shot out from my hands to meet the flames, which exploded into a cold mist on impact.

Sevryn's eyes widened, then narrowed at me. *"Interesting."*

Jordan didn't try to hide his shocked stare, though his expression also carried relief.

Suddenly I realized Kaizyn was no longer standing beside me.

I caught a flicker of Vyrthil, sneaking up behind Sevryn through the crowd.

Sevryn tracked my glance, and his lips spread slowly into a smile.

Dread washed through me.

"Well, this has been fun," Sevryn said, "but I'm getting bored." He reached out a hand. "Madison?"

I turned to find Madison right next to me, her eyes wide with panic.

I noticed her trembling hand holding a knife—just in time to feel her plunge it into my chest.

# CHAPTER 25
# TAKE YOUR THRONE

*Jordan*

My body wouldn't move. Every second stretched out like an eternity. A shout tore from deep inside me as I watched Madison drive the knife into Ayla's chest.

Ayla's eyes shot wide with shock and pain.

Madison stood stock-still but sobbing as Ayla's body crumpled to the ground.

From the corner of my eye, I saw Kaizyn drop, too.

The fire-cat collapsed beside him. His flames winked out.

Something inside me snapped.

Time rebounded like a slingshot set loose, and my body shot with it—straight into Sevryn.

My hands closed around his throat.

Sevryn let out a strangled gasp as he fought me. "How are you—Get off me! Guards!"

"You killed her!" The screams burst from me, feral and furious. "You *killed* her!"

I saw only him, only Sevryn's icy, wide eyes and pale face—and I wanted him *dead.*

The rune on my arm surged bright. Heat shot through my veins and out through my hands.

Sevryn shrieked in pain as my flames seared his face. "Attack him! Attack him!"

Darklings poured down from the city walls.

Screams of terror broke out from the villagers.

Guards clamped down on my arms and shoulders from multiple directions. They yanked me off Sevryn and threw me to the ground. One guard drove his knee into my back while others held my legs and arms, pinning me. My face was the only part they weren't holding down, but it still dug hard into the dirt ground. I could barely breathe.

Panicked villagers rushed past me in every direction, some of them dropping as the darklings took them down.

A voice screamed for me. "Jordan! She's still breathing! Etcher! Please, *someone*, help!"

I wrenched my face toward the voice. *Madison.* Tears streamed down her face. She cradled Ayla against her on the ground.

My chest clenched with a new wave of panic.

A few yards away, Sevryn staggered to his feet.

But I cared only about Ayla.

"Etcher! Maxim!" I strained to see the gallows, uncertain whether they were still chained up. "Someone help her, *please!*"

Sevryn's boot landed inches from my face. He knelt down and yanked my chin up to look at him.

Pain shot through my neck.

Chaos swam all around us—people running, screaming, darklings shrieking in victory as they dropped bodies to the ground.

Sevryn shook my face, forcing my eyes to his. There was murder in his glare. "No one is coming to help *any* of you."

The air split open, and a mob of flame-tossing, sword-slinging Ley-Guards poured out of it.

Striker slammed into Sevryn like a golem of living flame, knocking him away from me.

His partner, Brone, rushed up behind him, dropping darklings around me right and left with shots from a glowing pistol.

"Jordan!" The familiar voice made my heart catch.

"*Mom?*"

The *zing* of a runed arrow shot past my head, and the guard on my back fell away. The other guards dropped me, pulled into their own battles.

I jumped up as my mother sprinted up to me. "Jordan! Oh—your face!"

I grabbed her hand. "Ayla—please, Mom, help me!" I dragged her to where Madison still cradled Ayla and dropped to my knees beside them. "Ayla. *Ayla?*"

She was limp in Madison's lap, head tipped back, her breaths shallow, her face far too pale. A splotch of blood was quickly spreading across her chest.

Madison's terrified eyes locked on mine. "What do we do?"

A wiry hand clamped my shoulder. "Give her to me."

I looked up to see Etcher behind me.

"Quickly," he said. "There isn't much time."

There was something wild in his eyes. I hesitated.

"Varias Burgild!" A voice thundered through the chaos.

I turned.

Maddox Rogers strode toward me wearing battle leathers in a style I'd seen only in Hub archives. His eyes were cold with fury. He was still old and thin, but as dirt swirled in a whirlwind around him—his Fortis magic, wind magic—he looked every bit the hero of his own legend.

He raised his hands, and the sandstorm around him intensified as his glare locked on Etcher behind me. "Get *away* from my granddaughter."

Etcher yanked his hand from me and jumped back. "I was trying to help. A rune. For healing!"

Reina and Maxim Warwick, the apothecarist from the gallows, rushed up beside me as Etcher and Maddox stared each other down.

Relief filled me at the sight of Reina—and of Champ, waggling beside her. But it didn't last long.

"Give the girl to me, quickly," Maxim Warwick told me.

Shouts of battle, zinging arrows, pistol shots, and the darklings' feral shrieks still rang out all around us, but my world centered on Ayla.

Reina slid in, her face grim as her gaze fell on Ayla. She glanced at Maxim, then put her hand on my shoulder. "Maddox said we can trust him."

I slid back so Maxim could reach Ayla.

He yanked vials from his pockets and poured them onto Ayla's chest.

I tore my gaze away from her and scooted back to give them room.

Champ pivoted to my side, tense, scanning the surrounding chaos.

"Why are you here?" Maddox growled from behind me, his furious glare still locked on Etcher.

"I was helping!" Etcher yelled again. He took a couple of nervous steps back. His hands were trembling. "I've been nothing but a friend to the boy, like I vowed. Nothing but a help and a friend!"

Maddox flicked his gaze to me. "Is that true?"

"Yes. I think—" I stared up at Maddox as Madison sobbed quietly beside me and Ayla. "What's—"

Maddox spun back toward Etcher. "Varias Burgild, I release you of your vow!"

Maddox's eyes suddenly glassed over. He staggered backward, like an invisible fist had struck him.

Etcher's head slung back, his spine arched, and an inhuman shriek escaped from his throat. His body trembled, then his old man form morphed, tripling in size as his spindly arms sped into bulky, muscled limbs. Wide, dark wings exploded from his back, shredding his tunic.

Champ let out a low growl.

I stared up at Etcher and gasped. "You're an ArcFae."

He flicked dark, glinting eyes in my direction. A tattooed cluster of intricate, runed symbols covered the ArcFae's torso, forming the shape of a treasure chest in a field of flowers that wrapped around his sides. His ribs heaved in heavy breaths. The tattoos were rapidly fading.

Across from him, Maddox straightened, his eyes clearer than ever. His glance cut to me, then back to Etcher. "I remember."

"I've kept my vow," Etcher—or Varias, or whoever he was—spoke deeply now, his voice resonant and inhuman. "I protected your secrets, and the boy."

"You must have," Maddox said, calmer, "or you'd be dead right now. Those were the terms."

"Indeed," Varias said.

"Then you are free."

Varias nodded once, then launched into the sky and flew off.

"He's *leaving* us?" Madison yelled.

From somewhere in the distance, I heard Sevryn let out a chilling, maniacal laugh.

Brone rushed up. "The magic is weakening. Darklings are scrambling to find a way into the tunnels where the palace vault is hidden. The wards won't hold much longer."

Striker joined him. "More darklings are approaching from the mountains. We've hidden the people in the citadel, but—"

His speech was interrupted as several darklings barreled into him and Brone.

My parents and Reina's parents rushed in to help them.

I moved closer to Ayla, beside Maxim.

Madison and Reina scooted back to give me room.

Maddox hurried over, taking position on Ayla's other side.

Maxim climbed to his feet, glaring down at Maddox. "Enough is enough. We have to get him to the vault!"

"No time!" Maddox yelled back, staring up at him. "Help Ayla first!"

"There's no time for *any* of this!" Striker growled as he slung his flame whip into a new mob of darklings. "Just do it, Maddox!"

"No! You can't do it *here*!" Maxim yelled. "The darklings—he's too exposed!"

I stared between them in confusion. Were they talking about Kaizyn?

"It's my vow, and that's *my* granddaughter!" Maddox shot to his feet, his fists clenched. "I'll *do* what needs *done*!"

Behind me, Ayla gasped.

I spun toward her, all other conversation forgotten.

Her eyes shot open.

"Ayla!" The others jumped out of my way.

"Jordan?"

"I'm here." Ayla stared up at me as I pulled her into my arms and brushed some hair back from her face.

Her eyes locked on mine for one perfect moment—then they rolled back and she dropped limp.

"It's not working!" Maxim cried, lunging in again to examine Ayla.

I heard Maddox yell, and swirls of wind kicked up again, battering us with sand as he fought back a group of darklings.

Reina's dad rushed up beside us. "I've got Kaizyn." He lowered him to the ground, then raised an arm to protect his face from the sandstorm.

Maxim hovered his hands over both Ayla's and Kaizyn's chests. "We're losing them." He yanked more vials from his pocket. "Come on, come on!"

Darklings crashed into both of us and yanked Ayla from my arms.

"No!" I lunged after them, but more darklings swooped in, battering my face. "Ayla!"

Flames shot from my hands and the darklings pulled back, shrieking.

Champ snapped and growled, but a large darkling knocked him aside with a hard kick.

I heard him yelp as he fell. "Champ!"

Sand and wind swirled around us as Maddox fought back, but more darklings swept in, grappling with Reina and the others.

Reina made it to Champ and crouched over him, slashing at the swooping darklings with her dagger. "Go!" she shouted to me. "Get Ayla!"

I stumbled to my feet and rushed after the ones who had taken Ayla—only to run smack into Sevryn, holding Ayla's limp body against his chest with one arm.

Sevryn grinned menacingly as he closed one clawed hand around Ayla's throat. "They say, when you want something done right—"

I lunged for him.

Sevryn's magic clamped around me again like an iron fist.

I dropped to my knees in mid-leap.

Sevryn's grin widened as he raised his free hand toward me.

"No!" I fought him every inch, body trembling from resistance, but still my hand raised against my will, flames crackling over my fingers as they angled toward Ayla's bloodied chest.

From somewhere in the distance, Reina screamed. "Jordan!"

Maddox Rogers rushed toward us in a whirlwind of sand, sending all the darklings in his path flying. His eyes locked on me. "Cathal-Reigar, son of Veilar!" he yelled from within the sandstorm. "*Take your throne!*"

Something snapped in my chest, like a dam breaking.

Fire surged through my veins.

# Chapter 26

# The Rightful King

*Striker*

I had just incinerated one darkling and yanked my knife from another's lifeless chest when the air in the market exploded with heat.

I looked up to see Jordan engulfed in flames—and raging. His one good eye looked crazed. Staring at him now, for the first time, I could see it—the Fae king he truly was.

The darklings around him yelped and scattered.

Sevryn cowered back from him. "What—what are you—" His eyes went cold, and he slashed his claws across Ayla's throat.

She dropped to the ground.

"No, kid!" I yelled, kicking darklings out of the way as I tried to get to them.

Maddox Rogers dove in, cradling his granddaughter's body to his chest. I could hear his wail even over the fighting.

A guttural, feral roar burst from Jordan's throat. "Nooooo!"

Fire exploded from his chest.

I staggered back as the wave hit me, then as quick as it had come, it vanished.

I straightened.

Every Dark Fae in the square—including Sevryn—had burst into clouds of ash.

Jordan stood, staring at Ayla's fallen body, like a statue of living flame.

Brone and I gaped at each other over the ashy clouds in the sudden silence.

I glanced around the market square. All the LeyGuards were still standing... but not a single Dark Fae had survived. What kind of power did this kid *have*?

Jordan's flames wicked out.

I made it to his side just as he dropped to the ground beside Ayla.

He reached for her. "No," he whispered, then dropped his hand.

The ground trembled.

Brone rushed up beside me. "Striker," he said, his voice urgent.

I looked up.

A dark cloud was racing in from the distance.

"More darklings," Brone muttered, then glanced at me. "Far too many of them."

The tremors in the ground intensified.

Maddox clutched Ayla to his chest, but his eyes snapped up to Jordan, whose gaze had gone glassy.

"Jordan!" He reached one hand out, shaking him. "Jordan!"

Jordan forced his gaze up to Maddox, and the tremors stopped. But the pain on Jordan's face made my chest clench.

"Look!" Maddox said, and shifted Ayla.

The wound on her neck was closing.

"Maxim's faespells are still working," Maddox said, shaking Jordan's arm again. "It's not too late. There's still hope—for her *and* Kaizyn. We need to get them to the vault."

"The vault?" Jordan looked dazed.

"Yes," Maddox said. "I need you to open it."

"Open—I can't—" His gaze cleared, but he looked no less confused.

I stepped up beside them. "You're the real prince of Teionyr, kid."

"*What?*" His wide stare flicked up to me.

I shrugged. "I don't make the rules."

Jordan turned his wide stare back on Maddox as his parents and the rest of the LeyGuards rushed up to join us, along with the dog.

Reina had her arm around Madison, who looked close to having a breakdown. Reina's face twisted in grief as she caught sight of Ayla.

"It's true," Maddox told Jordan.

Jordan's dad stepped toward him. "It's true," he echoed, and his eyes locked on Jordan's. A long, heavy moment passed between them.

A cacophony of darkling shrieks echoed off the mountains above the city—they were almost here.

"The vault!" Maddox shouted, and Jordan seemed to snap out of it.

He scurried to his feet. "O-Okay. How do I get there?"

Jordan's dad gripped his shoulder. "I'll go with you."

"Let's all go," Maxim said, glancing at the sky. "Nobody wants to be caught out here when *those* things land."

"I've got the girl." I knelt and scooped up Ayla.

Brone did the same for Kaizyn.

Reina's mom helped Maddox to his feet. "Do you remember the way?"

Maddox nodded, his eyes sharp as knives. "I remember *everything*. Let's go. Someone grab Kaizyn's fire-cat, too."

Reina's dad rushed off to find Vyrthil.

T he vault was hidden in a labyrinth of dark tunnels beneath the palace.

Our small group jogged through the tunnels as best we could without Brone, Reina's dad, or me jostling our unconscious charges too much. Those of us who could wield flame—myself, Jordan, and his parents—cast small fire-orbs to hover beside us for light.

Champ trailed along beside Jordan, who didn't say a word the whole time.

Not that I could blame him. There was a lot to process.

As we jogged, Maddox explained, breathing heavily. "The vault contains a pool of healing. It's our best chance—maybe our only one." He glanced back at Ayla in my arms. "*If* we get there in time. They're still linked, so if either dies..." His voice trailed off. He didn't need to finish.

Jordan picked up the pace, urging Maddox forward.

It was a good thing Maddox remembered the way, because we could've starved down there before we ever found the right tunnels by accident. With Maddox leading, we made it to the vault in minutes.

The last tunnel we took dead-ended into the vault door. The door was at least eight feet tall, made of either metal or some kind of shiny stone far too thick to break through, and carved with intricate Teionyrian runes.

"You're up," Maddox said to Jordan. "No one but the rightful king or queen of Teionyr can open this door."

Jordan froze. "I'm not—"

His father clasped his shoulder. "You are now. All the previous kings are dead."

Jordan was clearly still in shock. He shook his head. "What if I can't—"

"You can," Maddox said, glancing at Ayla in my arms. "You will. To save *her*. Yes?"

Jordan sucked a sharp breath, then placed his hand on the door.

Every rune in the door surged with white-hot light.

Jordan yanked his hand back, shaking it. "That stung."

Maddox nudged the door, and it swung open. He smiled at Jordan. "You did it."

For a moment, we all just stared.

Jordan really *was* the true prince, the now-king of Teionyr.

Then we rushed inside.

The vault was like an underground cavern, its rock ceiling about twenty feet high and lit by magical orbs overhead, with a glistening, natural spring bubbling up in the center of the floor—sourced from who-knew-where, though I was certain the same magic that had sealed the door protected anything from swimming in without authorization. Shelves full of vials and jars of all kinds of magical ingredients lined the cavern walls, along with more than enough jewels and ornate golden objects to buy a large Earthside island.

Maddox hurried us to the pool in the center. "Put them here."

Brone and I lowered Ayla and Kaizyn next to the pool's edge, and Reina's dad laid Vyrthil beside them.

"I've been here only once before," Maddox said, turning to Jordan. "With Kaizyn. The baby was injured in our escape, and the King and I brought him here to heal him." His eyes settled on Jordan. "Veilar knew Kaizyn was not the true heir—but he took him in as his own. With his blessing, I took you Earthside. He meant to come for you, when you came of age—to give you the *choice* of whether you returned. If not, he would've done the ceremony to cement Kaizyn as the rightful king. Either way, he loved you *both*."

Jordan's dad squeezed his shoulder.

Jordan nodded, then glanced at Kaizyn. "So he's... basically my brother?"

Maddox nodded. "Yes."

A mix of emotions played over Jordan's face as he took that in.

Rapid footsteps sounded from the tunnels outside, and all of us spun toward the door, weapons and magic at the ready.

Callan rushed in. "Keyja found an active portal to the closest village. The people hiding in the citadel told me you'd come in here, and I came as fast as I—"

"Callan!" Madison ran toward him and fell into his arms.

He hugged her tight to his chest, then searched her face. "Are you all right?"

She nodded. "Yes, but—"

Callan's eyes fell on Ayla and Kaizyn, and he tensed. "What happened?"

"Something we're trying to undo," Maddox said. "Hurry. Grab Jordan's arm."

"What?" Callan said.

"Jordan's the true prince of Teionyr, Kaizyn and Ayla are dying, and apparently Jordan summoning some kind of royal magic from this watery hole in the floor is the only thing that can save them," I said. "Caught up now?"

Callan stared at me, but to his credit, he then jumped right into action. He squeezed Madison's hand quickly, then left her and hurried toward the pool. "What do we need to do?"

"Only a seated royal can call the pool's magic," Maddox continued. "We have to finish Jordan's coronation rites. Jordan, you need to summon your sear-bind, and pray with everything you've got that it's something that can heal. The more powerful, the better—though how strong your sear-bind is will depend on the strength of *your* magic. If you don't get one that can heal, we can try to use the pool's magic directly, but we'll cross that bridge if we reach it. Quickly, kneel here. I've seen it done. I'll coach you through it." He pointed at a spot near the pool. "Maxim, Callan, hold his arms, make sure he doesn't fall in." Maddox yanked a dusty book from a shelf and hurried back to the pool.

Jordan dropped to his knees and started praying as the other two moved up next to him.

"He can summon a sear-bind outside the Wilds?" Callan asked.

Maxim stared at him. "Where do you think this pool comes from? It's for emergencies, only, but—no matter, grab that arm."

Jordan glanced over at Ayla. "Will she and Kaizyn be okay?"

Callan stiffened, then glanced between Maddox and Maxim. "You should probably know—Keyja intensified their bond. She had to, for Kaizyn to leave the Veil. They're fully entwined now."

"*Entwined*?" Maxim's eyes widened. "Did Ayla agree to that?"

"Yes, but only to save him," Callan said, nodding to Jordan.

"Entwined," Maxim muttered again.

"What does that mean?" Jordan asked.

"If we don't do this ceremony, it won't mean anything!" Maddox snapped. "They're *dying*. Focus, and we can figure out the rest later!"

Jordan stiffened. "Tell me what to do."

Maddox shut his eyes and tipped his head back. "Please God, favor us. Send your protection!" Then he flopped the book open, sending up a cloud of dust, and locked his gaze on Jordan. "Repeat after me, and when I tell you, plunge your hands into the pool. The words will be in Teionyrian. Just repeat them exactly as I say them."

"Wait, what will I be saying?" Jordan asked.

"You're pledging to be an honest and trustworthy king for all your life, and never to harm your people."

Jordan hesitated. "I don't even know these people. What if—"

Maddox's face softened. "*You* are one of these people. Callan is one of these people. Ayla is bonded to Kaizyn, now—so *she*... is one of these people. They're a good people, Jordan. They just need a decent king."

Jordan swallowed, then nodded. "Read. I'll do it."

Maddox tipped his face to the book. "Vera—"

Inhuman shrieks echoed from the tunnels.

"Shut the vault door!" Maddox screamed.

Brone and I raced toward it, but darklings were already pouring in.

Reina, Champ, and Reina and Jordan's parents rushed up behind us and fought the creatures back as Brone and I leaned all our weight against the door, trying to force it shut against the writhing, shrieking pile of darklings clawing to break through.

"How did they get in through the tunnel wards?" Maxim yelled.

"Veras vesim moras," Maddox called out over the darklings' shrieks.

"Veras vesim moras," Jordan shouted after him.

Several darklings squirmed free into the vault, and were met with flames from Reina's parents.

"Hurry!" Reina screamed as she slashed another one back.

"How did they even *get* here without us hearing them in the tunnels? It doesn't make sense!" Brone yelled.

He was right. This many darklings couldn't have moved in total silence. We should've heard them long before they reached the door.

Brone and I braced as a fresh wave of darklings slammed into the door.

I shot a column of flame out through the door's crack, but as soon as those darklings crumpled to ash, more took their place. The tunnel must've been *flooded* with them. We were barely holding our ground, and making no headway toward actually getting the door closed.

"These things are strong," Brone grunted.

"Arvas kalix sarventum!" Maddox shouted.

"Arvas kalix sarv—"

The door flung open, slamming Brone and me back into the cavern wall. A group of darklings poured into the vault like a thrashing, black river.

I shoved the heavy door off of me and closed it as much as I could against the roiling darkling horde trying to break through.

The others ran up to help with the darklings that had made it into the vault.

Blood ran from my nose where the door had crashed into it. I wiped it away. "Brone?"

He was on the floor.

"*Brone*?" I rushed toward him, blocking him with my body as Ley-Guards and darklings frenzied around us.

Flames shot past me as Jordan's parents tried to fight some of the darklings back.

Reina's parents leaned their weight into the door, bottlenecking the stream of darklings—but some still snuck through and as quickly as Reina and Jordan's parents slashed at and charred them or Champ tore into them, more poured into the gap, pressing to get inside the vault.

"Arvas kalix sarventum," I heard Jordan call out.

Brone stirred, and I helped him up.

"I'm good," Brone said, though he looked terrible. He drew his pistol and spun back toward the door, dropping darklings as they came through the doorway.

I lassoed and fricasseed others with my flames.

Still more came, trampling over each other to get in.

"We're out of time!" I yelled.

"Melos vercin arvelum!" Maxim shouted.

"Melos vercin arvelum!" Jordan echoed.

"Put your hands in the water!" Maddox yelled, followed by a splash.

A shock wave burst through the cave.

It knocked *all* of us back, including the darklings, but they quickly returned to their feet and lunged again.

Jordan and Maddox had gone quiet.

"How's it going back there?" I yelled, as another wave of darklings surged at us.

A rumble trembled through the vault floor.

"Ha ha!" I heard Maddox yell.

Madison screamed.

A torrent of white-hot flame arced over my head, slamming into the darkling army.

It swept through them, turning row after row of them to ash, all the way out through the doorway.

The darklings remaining in the tunnel shrieked and fled.

I sighed in relief. "Good going, kid." I turned, expecting to see Jordan still blazing behind me—and my match nearly fell from my mouth.

Jordan crouched protectively in front of Ayla, no flames in sight.

But behind him, hunched to fit beneath the twenty-foot ceiling, wings scraping the cavern walls—was a shimmering red dragon, still dripping pool-water on the cavern floor.

A breath of smoke puffed from its mouth as it lowered its head to Jordan's height. Its nose was bigger than his entire body.

Jordan glanced back at it over his shoulder, staring into its enormous eyes. "Please," was all he said.

The dragon nodded, then reached its face past him and pressed its nose to Ayla's chest.

Ayla's body surged gold with light—and Kaizyn's glowed in response.

"Yes, yes!" Maddox shouted, clapping his hands. "It's working!"

Beside him, Maxim and Callan both stared at Jordan in silent awe.

The dragon removed its snout from Ayla's chest.

Champ slunk near, seeming nervous, but the dragon tilted its head at him and he perked right up, then trotted to Jordan's side.

Ayla stirred, and Maddox rushed toward her. "It's all right. I'm here."

"Jordan?" Ayla muttered as Maddox helped her sit up.

Jordan grabbed her hand. "We're *both* here."

"Kaizyn!" Callan rushed to Kaizyn's side and helped him sit, too.

Kaizyn and Ayla looked at each other, their gazes locking as something intense passed between them.

From the look on Jordan's face, he noticed it, too.

"Ayla!" Reina dashed up, sheathing her dagger, and wrapped Ayla in a hug. "I'm *so* glad you're okay."

Reina pulled back, and Ayla's eyes finally caught on the creature over Jordan's shoulder.

Ayla gasped and scurried back. "What—*Jordan?*" Her wide, shocked gaze flicked back to him.

Kaizyn's stare locked on it, too, and his face went pale.

Rapid footsteps slapped toward the vault door. "Master Callan!"

We all turned as a Fae child rushed up to the vault entrance, wearing servant's clothes. He stopped respectfully at the door. "Master Callan! The monsters are gone! I brought the people into the palace, as you said, but—"

He stopped mid-sentence as he saw the dragon. His mouth fell open.

Behind him, more and more wide-eyed Teionyrian faces of all ages gathered at the vault door.

Ayla glanced at Kaizyn, but only for a moment before she turned back to Jordan.

"*Jordan?*" she asked again.

Jordan blushed, then ran a hand over the back of his neck. "I—um—"

Kaizyn turned to stare at Callan, who seemed at a loss for words.

Maddox wrapped his arm around Ayla, then absent-mindedly patted Kaizyn's arm as an awkward silence fell over the room.

"Oh, for heaven's sake, is no one gonna—" Reina rolled her eyes, then spun to Ayla and gestured excitedly. "Jordan is the rightful king of Teionyr, he killed all the Dark Fae with a blast of flame, and now he's sear-bound to a *dragon!*"

# Epilogue One: Not Even a Prince

*Kaizyn*

Ayla and I were still bonded. I felt her heart surge as she looked at Jordan, and when she spotted his dragon—then her pity, when Callan confirmed I was not truly a prince of Teionyr.

No wonder I had summoned such a common, average sear-bind.

Jordan, on the other hand, had summoned the very sear-bind Father had hoped for, the one he knew could save our kingdom.

Ayla didn't want to be linked to me in the first place. Now, we discovered I was not even a prince. I meant no more than the next man in the town streets. She had saved my life for no reason.

And she was stuck with me.

I glanced at the door to the vault.

My people stood there, watching our tense assembly with expressions of awe and pity. Were they happy to have a new king? Fates knew I had failed them, in more ways than one. *My people.* It was still true, but in a much different way than I'd been raised to believe. Were they still my responsibility, now that we all knew I was nothing but a servant used to protect the real prince? Somehow, I still felt responsible.

Father would've known what to do, how to handle this with honor... but he wasn't truly my father, either, was he?

Everything I'd been raised to believe was a lie.

Ayla tore her wide eyes from Jordan's—with hesitation, as I clearly felt—and turned to me. "Kaizyn."

I could feel her friendship, her concern for me... and her longing to be with Jordan. Her excitement and relief at being near him again. Her awe at his magic. Her regret that she was bonded to me. Her sense of duty to me, that had even made her look at me at all.

Friendship. Duty. Not love. It wasn't her fault; I'd known going in. I'd intensified our bond only to save *him*, to save her heart from breaking—and we'd succeeded. We'd saved her precious Jordan. And thank the fates we had, because he was the savior of our kingdom, the true king of Teionyr!

What did that make me?

"Kaizyn?" Ayla reached for me, eyes full of concern—heart full of pity and regret.

Jordan held out his hand. "Kaizyn. It's an honor to meet you."

I should've greeted Jordan and his magnificent dragon with the respect they deserved. I should've thanked him for saving my life—and Ayla's. I should have welcomed him as the brother he apparently was, as the rescue he was for my people, and bowed to him as my new king.

I just wanted to be alone.

I jumped to my feet. "I need a moment."

Vyrthil, now stirring as my own power returned, rose to his feet beside me, tense, his keen eyes focused on the dragon.

Ayla's emotions rushed toward me as she looked up at me—guilt, sorrow, concern, pity... hope. Her eyes glinted with an echo of my pain, emotions reverberating between us and amplifying. "Maybe there's still a way," she said, "some magic that could undo this. So you—so we can both—be free."

I was standing with the pieces of my broken heart, while she thought of how to be rid of me.

I hurried toward the vault door.

Vyrthil flamed and fell in step beside me.

"Kaizyn!" Callan called after me, but no one but Vyrthil followed me as I ran for the tunnel.

"Let them go," I heard Jordan say softly.

The Teionyrians at the door parted to let us through, already following the commands of their new king. They averted their gazes as I rushed past, all but the children, who stared at me.

Their eyes were full of pity, too.

# EPILOGUE TWO: THE DARK KING MARCHES

***Rory***

It was bad enough I got left behind while Callan went off to save my sister and her friends, but sitting in the grass eating a bowl of unidentified stew made by a scary Fae woman with a ball of lightning in her chest was not my idea of a good time.

Not that I wasn't grateful she'd saved my life. I was. But the extended silence was getting *really* awkward.

I poked my spoon at the remaining bits of my stew. "This was good. Thank you."

Keyja leaned back on her hands and glanced up at me. "You're welcome." Crackles of lightning snapped from her chest.

I tore my eyes away, then turned to the giant celery nearby. He hadn't moved since Callan had rushed off, and Keyja had made no attempt to talk to him and no mention of him saying anything—not that I'd be able to hear him if he did—which seemed kind of rude, to me. I stared up at his waving leaves. "So, you're, like... a talking tree?"

Keyja stared wide-eyed at me, but either the tree said nothing in response or she didn't care to share what he said.

I tried to brush off the judgment in her expression. "Any word from the others?"

Keyja shook her head. "Mraugathal is watching. If word comes, I will let you know."

I scraped my spoon on the sides of the wooden bowl. "Callan should have let me go with him. I could've helped."

Keyja's voice softened. "He wishes to protect you. Your sister means a lot to him, and therefore, so do you."

I adjusted my position, feeling the ache in my back and shoulder and ribs, and sighed. "Yeah. Okay."

I knew I wasn't any kind of special trained warrior or whatever, but—I just wished I didn't need to be *protected*. Talk about jabbing at a man's ego.

I was grateful for Callan and Striker and Keyja saving my life, but after Callan left me behind like a helpless child with my Fae babysitter, any remaining pride I'd had was trampled and left begging for mercy. I would have chased Callan through the portal and insisted on going, if every breath I took didn't feel like knives in my chest. I'd only made it ten steps. That was the worst part—I knew he was right. I'd have been a liability.

Mraugathal's leaves danced violently, and Keyja suddenly sat bolt upright.

"Word has just come. There was a great battle in the market in Teionyr. Many of Mraugathal's cousins in the market square were destroyed—" She met my eyes. "Many died. Plants and otherwise."

My breath caught. "Madison? The others?"

"They live," Keyja said.

Breath escaped me in relief.

"But Ayla and Kaizyn were gravely injured."

My heart lurched.

Keyja's eyes went glassy. "Callan arrived a little while ago. He headed into the palace..." She squinted, as though trying to focus, then her eyes cleared. "That is all. They descended into the vaults, and Mraugathal has no cousins there. We cannot see what is happening."

Mraugathal's leaves shook violently again.

"Wait," Keyja said, eyes glassy again. "The people are chattering outside the palace. Something has—" Her eyes cleared, and she stared at me in shock. "Jordan has summoned a dragon!"

I gaped. "He's summoned a *what*?"

Keyja grinned. "Ayla and Kaizyn are safe. The battle is won for now. And with a dragon on Teionyr's side, Upper Faeside may finally stand a—" Keyja's eyes shot wide.

She jumped to her feet and stared up at Mraugathal, whose branches were waving wildly.

"How soon?" she asked with a quiver in her voice. She waited a moment, then her entire face went pale, and she lunged for me. "Come! Hurry!" She grabbed my arm and yanked me to my feet with startling strength.

She dropped my arm and dashed for the cottage.

My bowl clattered to the ground as I stumbled after her, trying to ignore the pain in my side. "Why? What's happening?"

She spun to me as we reached the door. "The Dark King marches from Morrowen as we speak, with an army of darklings and Selkblood commanders. He intends to breach the LeyGuard Hub. From there, he can take any LeyGate he wishes, and pour his army straight into the allied Fae towns." She grabbed a satchel from a hook on the wall and began shoving supplies into it.

"That's horrible," I said. "What can we do?"

"You don't understand. They're coming through *here* to do it. We're the most direct path."

I felt the blood drain from my face. "Oh."

Keyja shoved the satchel into my arms, then forced a stone etched with symbols into my hand. "Go through the portal to the Hub. That stone will open the Gate at the east barrier of the dome. Warn the LeyGuard. Go! Quickly!"

I stared at her. "Aren't you coming?"

Keyja's chest crackled. "I have to defend Arcvale."

"By *yourself*?"

A beam of blinding light surged out of Keyja's chest, and suddenly I was staring at a massive, crackling, electrical bison that nearly reached the cottage ceiling. Its dark eyes locked on me as it stood beside Keyja, and I fought the urge to scream like a frightened child.

Keyja grabbed my arm. "I have Tofa. I'll be fine." She shoved me out the door and pointed out an archway I could just make out across the field. "Now go! They need your warning!"

Her last statement startled me back to reality. I nodded. "Don't worry. I've got this." I gripped the satchel under one arm and ran for the Gate with everything I had.

# READ THE REST OF THE SERIES!

**END OF BOOK 2**

(To be continued in Book 3, *Fae Curses, Dark Kings, and Other Things That Must Fall.*)

**Read the rest of this trilogy!**

*L*eyGuards, Faespells, and Other Things That Breach the Veil is Book 2 of a trilogy, and Book 3 is already available for order! Grab Book 3 now at the link below!

*Fae Curses, Dark Kings, and Other Things That Must Fall* (The Leyward Stones, Book 3): **https://books2read.com/ faecurses**

## Did you know there will be more Leyward Stones books to come, too?

The *Macchiatos/LeyGuards/Fae Curses* trilogy is Trilogy 1 of The Leyward Stones series, but Trilogy 2 is already in the works! Subscribe to my newsletter at **http://ccrawfordwriting.com/subscribe** to get updates on my future releases!

# Acknowledgements

A sincere thank you my family, without whom none of my writing would be possible.

Thank you again to M.J., to Christy, to the rest of my Alpha team, to Lydia, to Candice, to my Patreon and PirateCat subscribers, to the Wulf Pack and DreamForge and my Vella readers and Vella author friends, and everyone else who supported the months of creation of this book and/or helped me promote it in its original serial format and again at the release of this revised, updated form in e-book and paperback.

And thank you to God—ever and always—for His presence in every moment and every effort of every day... even the ones I spend venturing in the crazy worlds within my mind. I pray my books always bring Him glory, regardless of whatever else they may accomplish.

Want to see more from me, outside my published books? Come find me where I hang out online!

If you love **clean young adult fiction** and want a portal where you can read a bunch of my clean YA content, interact with me and other readers, and help me build a community around clean YA fiction, **check out my Story Subscribers portal on my website!** Find out more on the next page, or at **http://ccrawfordwriting.com/storysubscriberscontent**.

If you'd like to receive updates on future releases, behind-the-scenes info on my writing, and personal updates, subscribe to my monthly email newsletter at **http://ccrawfordwriting.com/subscribe**. I never spam my email subscribers—you can expect one email per month, with occasional bonus emails if I have a new release, sale, or something important to share. And you'll even get free story downloads for subscribing!

I'm also on social media! You can find me at:

Website: **http://ccrawfordwriting.com**

Blog: **http://ccrawfordwriting.com/blog**

Facebook: **http://facebook.com/ccrawfordwriting**

Instagram: **http://instagram.com/ccrawfordwriting**

YouTube: **http://youtube.com/ccrawfordwriting**

Or contact me directly through email at **ccrawford@ccrawfordwrit ing.com**. I'd love to see your comments and respond to any questions you might have.

Thank you so much for reading!

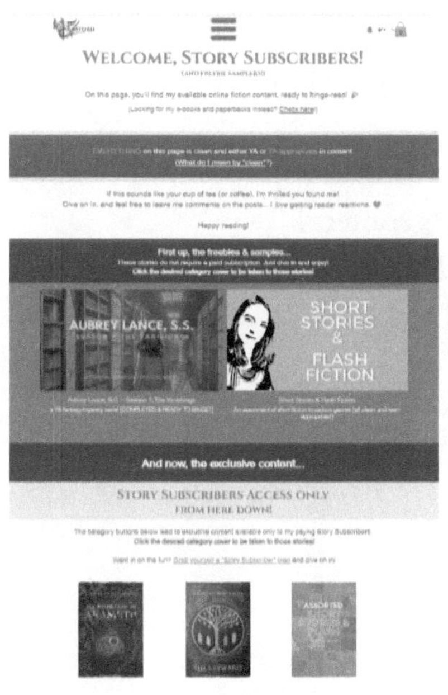

## Then check out my Story Subscribers portal!

It's a special section of my website where you'll find a collection of stories from me right there online & ready to binge-read! Some of the stories in there are free, and others are behind a small paywall... right now (as of May 2026), that paywall is only $1.99/month to access ALL of my Story Subscribers content. This small fee helps keep my business running... plus my Story Subscribers get access to some *exclusive* content not available anywhere else, like my ongoing serials and bonus side stories set in some of my published story worlds.

Also, EVERYTHING in my Story Subscribers portal is clean and either YA or YA-appropriate in content. **What do I mean by "clean"?** For me, that means:

PG-13 or less for violence (battle violence in the fantasy/sci-fi but no gratuitous gore).

Sweet/wholesome romance (when romance is present) that focuses on relationship and never goes beyond a chaste kiss.

NO profanity (but with an occasional mild euphemism like "dang" or similar, and occasional in-world, made-up "swear" words).

I write from a Biblical worldview (though much of my content is not explicitly religious), and do my best to portray healthy relationship dynamics, especially in parent-child relationships and romantic relationships, which I've found are often quite *unhealthy* in much of the mainstream YA fiction. My characters are not perfect, and do not always make the right choices, but their mistakes are always used for growth. There will always be a clear concept of good versus evil in my stories (especially fantasy!), and they'll always end with either a hard-fought happy ending, or at least a note of hope.

If this sounds like your cup of tea, I'm thrilled you found me—and I hope you'll check out my Story Subscribers content!

Just visit my Story Subscribers page at **http://ccrawfordwriting.com /storysubscriberscontent**to join or find out more!

Crystal Crawford writes clean YA fantasy and clean YA romance (and a smattering of other genres) in Florida, where every natural body of water hides something that could eat you, and if they don't get you, the weather might. She lives with her husband, five kids, two cats, one doofusy dog, and two live-in grandparents, who have all supported her dream of writing and drinking far too much coffee. Her imagination is her happy place! (But a deserted beach is nice, too.) When she isn't writing, she enjoys reading, napping, watching shows with her family, working in the garden, and homeschooling the kids, though most days you'll also find her doing laundry.

ALSO BY CRYSTAL CRAWFORD

**The Leyward Stones**

*Macchiatos, Faerie Princes, and Other Things That Happen at Midnight*
*LeyGuards, Faespells, and Other Things That Breach the Veil*
*Fae Curses, Dark Kings, and Other Things That Must Fall*
and more books to come!

**The Lex Chronicles (Legends of Arameth)**

*The Edge of Nothing*
*The Path to Paradox*
*The Ends of Exile*
and more books to come!

## Aubrey Lance, S.S. (Supernatural Sleuth)

Season 1: The Vanishings, now available to read in serial format in the forum on my website: http://ccrawfordwriting.com/forum/aubreylance -season1

## Secret Messages Sweet YA Romance Series

*I'm Not a Stalker*
*The Five Suspects*
and more books to come!

## Love and Aliens

*The Extraordinary, Extraterrestrial Love Lives of Doppelgangers*
and another book to come!

## Published Short Stories

- "Our Kind" (a Leyward Stones short story published in DreamForge Magazine) — available to read free at https://dreamforge.mywebportal.app/dreamforge/stories/show/our-kind-crystal-crawford

- "One Shot at Aeden" (a Leyward Stones short story published in DreamForge Magazine) — available to read free at https://dreamforge.mywebportal.app/dreamforge/stories/show/one-shot-at-aeden-crystal-crawford

- "Cheer Hawks and a Side of Murder" (a short story originally published in the Murderbirds anthology by Mike Jack Stoumbos)

- plus loads of other Leyward Stones, Legends of Arameth, and assorted short stories available inside PirateCat!

## Nonfiction

- The Unspoken Language: An Animal Trainer's Memoir

- Slap Him with a Fish: a Crash-Course in Fiction Writing

- Put Some Pants on That Kid: a Writing Handbook for High School and Beyond (Student Book and Parent/Teacher's Guide)

- The Other Side of the Law (a co-written lawyer's memoir)

- Unbreaking: How Giving Up Saved Our Marriage (a raw, real marriage memoir)

**Find the purchase links to many of the above books all in one place at**
http://ccrawfordwriting.com/books

www.ingramcontent.com/pod-product-compliance
Lightning Source LLC
Chambersburg PA
CBHW020034310726
48970CB00007B/2248